Fair Chase and Other Tales:

Grizzly Adventures, Wild Muskrats, Indian Guides and Lore, Lost Wives, Stag Attacks, Crashes, More!

Larry and Betty Roper

Big Mac Publishers – Sylacauga, Alabama
Printed and bound in the United States of America
www.bigmacpublishers.com

Author:	Larry (Laren) and Betty Roper
Editor:	Greg Bilbo
Cover and Interior Book Photos Copyright © 2011:	Larry Roper
Cover Illustration / Design:	Greg Bilbo
Proofreaders / Reviewers / Assistant Editors:	Leslie & DeeAnn Williamson

Scripture quotations taken from the "NASB," New American Standard Bible®, Copyright © 1960, 1962, 1963, 1968, 1971, 1972, 1973, 1975, 1977, 1995 by The Lockman Foundation. Used by permission. (www.Lockman.org)

Library of Congress Control Number: 2011907608

Library of Congress subject headings:

1. Adventures and Adventurers – Bibliography
2. Outdoor Life – Alaska
3. Hunting – Middle West
4. Fishing – Alaska
5. Adventure therapy.

BIASC / BASIC Classification Suggestions:

1. BIO023000   BIOGRAPHY & AUTOBIOGRAPHY / Adventurers & Explorers
2. SPO022000   SPORTS & RECREATION / Hunting
3. SPO014000   SPORTS & RECREATION / Fishing
4. OCC019000   BODY, MIND & SPIRIT / Inspiration & Personal Growth

ISBN-13: 978-0-9831983-5-2   ISBN-10: 0-9831983-5-7   V 1.0

Big Mac Publisher Book Titles may be purchased in bulk at great discounts and much cheaper than using normal channels by going directly through Big Mac Publishers. This is true for anyone, whether a retail vendor or for educational, business, fund-raising, spiritual or sales promotional purposes.

Big Mac Publishers, Sylacauga, Alabama – www.bigmacpublishers.com
Printed and bound in the United States of America

Fair Chase and Other Tales

Wilderness, which I define as the natural environment in the out-of-doors, is a unique laboratory that I believe is often used by God in developing character and enhancing relationships. I have found this especially true in the bonding of parents and children.

An airplane crash, a buck fight, a lost camera, and a grizzly bear encounter, along with other crazy adventures, were instrumental in the development and growth of the Roper family.

Additionally, throughout the book the biology and ecology of the animals are explained to showcase a delightful aspect of the world we live in.

Some comments from respected reviewers . . .

Intriguing tales of real life adventures by an avid sportsman, with his amazing wife, family, friends and Almighty God! -- April Seekins

True tales full of adventure, danger and suspense. How he stayed alive is a miracle. I am glad he did. Larry and Betty are the real deal! -- Larry Seekins

The first sentence of the introduction says it all, "*I think life should be an adventure*" Being an avid outdoorsman and a man of faith like Larry, I was completely captivated by "Fair Chase and Other Tales." Thank you for sharing your life and reliving exhilarating memories of days gone by. I only regret we didn't cross paths forty years ago. -- Pastor Zen Voorhies, Gering, Nebraska

I devoured every word. Josh did also. If you have never experienced wilderness camping or big game hunting, now is your chance without even leaving your easy chair. Larry and Betty made me feel as if I were right beside them all the way in their accounts. In fact I have been there a couple of times while Larry and I were co-students at Colorado State University and I know there is no exaggeration in these tales . . . *A great read.* -- Phil Lee

Dr. Roper has written a memoir that conveys God's presence in their lives. He gives you a taste of camping, fishing, and hunting including wildlife behavior and habitation . . . *a fast enjoyable read.* -- Diane Downer, Librarian

Larry and Betty, it has been a blessing to know you for these past 35 years. These are in spite of the "frozen toes," "parched tongue," "aching muscles," "heartburn" and "sleep depredation." God truly watched over you throughout all your adventurous life. Thanks for bringing these exciting times, so vividly alive, for the entire world to enjoy. -- Bill and Johnye Grebe

I enjoyed the descriptions of mountains and canyons, lakes and forests that you encountered during your trips into the wilderness. -- Paul Guillory

This book is a testimony to God's sovereignty and the everlasting value of faith, family and friends. -- Dianne Scribner

Table of Contents

Acknowledgements

Each person mentioned in this book deserves a big thank you. Without them, the book could not have been written. If it were not for their friendship we could not have shown the glory and power of God at work in our lives.

Also, my deepest gratitude goes to my patient wife and co-author. She put up with me through the years of hunting and fishing in the back country. She was instrumental in motivating me to write. A number of years ago she encouraged me to record many of these stories and others on a cassette recorder. That was a big help to get us started. Betty was the primary first hand of helps. As I wrote what I remembered she would go over it with great care and correct spelling, grammar, and flow of each event as well as provide input to the story, as she often remembered details I might leave out in recalling the story. Truly, she deserves the highest praise.

Each person we have written about or mentioned is a cherished, valued friend. Thanks to all.

Family moose hunt

Introduction

I think that life should be an adventure. Although it can be tragic at times or exhilarating at others, it should always be intriguing. I suggest that if the daily grind of modern existence has become mundane, then a great remedy is to give a moment's pause for an exploration, a look at the big picture of our incredible wilderness which conveys profound lessons, both large and small.

To live an adventuresome life, one need not survive airplane crashes or out-muscle rip tides. High adventure occurs in various forms all around us. It may be glimpsed under a leaf where a beetle is taking refuge from a predator, or it might be seen in the ever shifting "V" of geese flying overhead, being led to safe haven by a dauntless leader. We never know.

Life is tenuous yet precious and assails us with many twists and turns. Hardships and trials often become part of the fabric that matures us if we are receptive and willing to learn. Goals and dreams become possible. If not, we may end up going where we do not want to go, time after time. It has been said that if a person does not know where they want to go, well then, any old place will do—and that is usually nowhere.

Planning wilderness trips along with hunting, gathering, and fishing seem to lend to life a sense of direction and purpose—at least this has proven true for me and many companions. Being in the wilderness is taxing both mentally and physically. It has forced me to grow as a person in spiritual values as well as relationship skill building.

Perhaps this compilation of short stories will also highlight the significance of outdoor ethics and stimulate a desire to hone survival skills.

We have written this book to entertain, to show the myriad benefits of solid values, to teach outdoor skills, and to discuss our marvelous wildlife. Naturally, since the stories involve our family, the book cannot help but be autobiographical. We hope you enjoy our uniqueness as a family, who we are, and how we would like to be. Many have enjoyed the story telling about these adventures and urged us to write them down—so here they are.

May God bless you as you participate in these tales of adventure!

A death struggle

Chapter 1

Who Is Going to Die in North Park?

"Charlie! Look at that buck. He's caught in something. Look! Those two coyotes are waiting him out. You can just see the eagerness in those wild dogs. I bet they can taste venison right now."

Charlie nodded vigorously and pointed. Excitement was in his voice. "Over there on that knoll, an eagle. Hey! On that other hill, another eagle. They're playing the waiting game."

Before our eyes was a life and death struggle. We had topped out on a ridge in our U.S. Forest Service Jeep Wagoneer and had a perfect view. Our eyes took in a script that has probably been repeated and played throughout history yet seldom witnessed.

Two golden eagles, each sitting on parallel cone-shaped hills, were waiting and acting as sentinels for a grizzly scene between them.

1

The buck had won this fight but still faced grave danger.

A large buck mule deer was backing up with his antlers entangled in something. The two coyotes were circling the buck patiently waiting for the right moment to go in for the kill.

Through my 20-power spotting scope I saw that the antlers were locked with another buck's antlers. The second buck appeared dead and was being dragged around by the first. The dead buck appeared to be the largest but the live one was an old mossy horned buck that was still fighting for his life. The hind quarters of the dead buck were partially eaten, apparently by the two eager coyotes. The tiring buck was in deep trouble.

"We can help!" I said to Charlie. My voice portrayed intense excitement. "Let's get down there and see if we can set that old boy free."

"Boy, what a fight for survival this was," Charlie replied. "That buck has some reserve strength or he wouldn't be still standing and struggling."

I thought it was a bit late for the rut to still be going on as it was in early February. Normally, the peak of the breeding season takes place the last week in November through the first week in December. Bucks can and will breed a bit earlier than that if a doe starts into estrus, which is her heat period.

If a doe is not bred she will recycle in about 21 days, during which time she will ovulate another egg or eggs. This results in a high percentage of twins. Rarely are triplets born. However, twins are the most common in most mule deer herds in mature does. If a doe is not bred she will become receptive to the bucks again.

During the breeding season bucks stick close to does and fight off other bucks. Occasionally, they will be so aggressive they will harm each other or get their antlers locked together, as in this case. Studies in northern Colorado on reproduction show that nearly 100 percent of the females are bred each fall. Thus, this rutting behavior in February is unusual but not impossible.

Charlie and I were checking the habitat and forage utilization of the winter range for mule deer near Coalmont in North Park, Colorado. We were working that day, and yes, we got paid to go out and check on the deer herd. Great job, eh?

The day started out clear and cold with a new snow of about 8-12 inches on the ground. There had been a Chinook (a warm wind thawing the ground) creating a muddy condition. The snow had covered the mud, and it was soft and deep.

It was one of those glorious days to be out in big game country. Mountains around us stood out with clarity of color and excellent perception of depth. The scenery was on a level all its own.

It was 1964 and I was a young, budding wildlife biologist for the Routt National Forest and stationed in Steamboat Springs, Colorado. Charlie was the general district assistant with the North Park Ranger District in the Routt National Forest.

Charlie drove down the hill so we could set the monarch free. The coyotes slinked off into the sagebrush as we approached. Their behavior was typical scavenger/predator behavior. They could wait patiently for the victorious buck to succumb to the lack of food energy and exhaustion in order to feast on the carrion rather than risk injury by stepping in too quickly for a free meal.

We approached the scene, and the eagles lifted off to circle us in the clear blue sky. They registered their protest by incessant shrieking as they circled over the dramatic play. It has always been intriguing to me how skillfully eagles use their powerful wings, angling them just so and letting the wind carry

3

them closer. We had driven down and parked about 50 yards from the two deer.

The buck's antlers were hopelessly locked together.

I grabbed a double bitted ax from the vehicle and also got a camera. We walked to the entangled and subdued creature caught in nature's trap. We were pretty nonchalant and not very cautious at first.

That was probably because the poor fella didn't seem concerned about us, and he appeared to be exhausted. I snapped a couple of photos.

The next tricky step was to separate the two bucks—if we could figure out how. We had already decided we would probably have to chop the horns free. I was ready with the ax, so Charlie slowly approached the bucks from the side. The live buck looked complacent, but little did we know he was primed like a stick of TNT ready to explode at the slightest provocation, even though he looked harmless and tired.

Charlie carefully moved beside the buck up close to its head, then reached over the neck of the buck and grabbed the far side antler, while also holding tight to the near antler with his other hand. He looked like a cowboy getting ready to throw a steer. He even had his feet planted much the same way a

4

bulldogger does in a rodeo just before he starts to wrestle the animal to the ground.

Close up view of unusual locked antlers

A tine of the live buck was deep into the other's snout and thus worked like a steel clamp binding and locking the two deer together.

After studying the way the antler were entangled, I believed if I cut the muzzle off halfway to the eyes then it would release the tine and the binding effect it wielded. Subsequently, this would allow the victor to easily dislodge from his beaten foe altogether.

Charlie and the live buck were both facing me. Charlie was gripping the buck hard. I said, "I wonder what he'll do when I swing the ax?" I paused and then said, "Okay, Charlie, be ready for anything and hang on tight."

He replied, "Okay, I'm ready." I swung the ax and hit the mark squarely. Whoa! That buck reared back in total surprise, obviously trying to get away from not only the other deer but also Charlie and the ax. Charlie struggled very hard to subdue him.

"Are you ready for another try?" I asked.

"Yeah," he answered, "but be ready to help me hold him if you're able to get the nose cut into two pieces and if it frees him."

"I'm ready," I managed, through tight lips and gritted teeth. The words came out in short gasps as I was breathing hard and full of nervous tension.

I swung the ax back in preparation for another blow, but the buck was ready and reared before I was able to strike my target. I missed the nose and realized we might need a different approach. Charlie was once again wrestling the deer to hold him steady.

We thought for a minute and waited for the deer to calm down. We decided to give it another try. Time seemed to stand still for us, as we were so involved it was as if there was no such thing as time.

Charlie suggested, "Why don't you use shorter, less powerful chops instead of trying to make just one big cut. I think your swing is scaring the deer. He pulls back before you can deliver the blow."

"That's a good idea, Charlie!" So I began to hack with quick, short blows before the deer could respond. And it was working. In no time and with just a few hits, only skin was holding the nose together. The deer would be free momentarily. I realized that maybe I should get hold of the antlers and help Charlie out muscle the stag when this happened.

This was not easy to accomplish. I had to chop with one hand while holding the horns with the other. I put my hand on the ax handle up close to the ax head so I could be more accurate.

We were both relieved when I gave a final chop and the antlers came loose. I dropped the ax and used my newly freed hand to grasp onto the horns. Now Charlie and I had both hands on the buck's antlers. Charlie was on one side and I was on the other. Mr. Buck just stood there like a stunned criminal hit by an officer's stun gun.

Since he was just standing there and not fighting us or tossing his head, Charlie said, "Let's try just backing away and see if he stays put."

"Yeah, let's try it," I said. So Charlie and I let loose of the antlers and backed away. The buck looked dazed initially and didn't do anything—at first.

Charlie playfully picked up the ax by the handle and held the blade firmly pointed at the buck as if to say, "You stay away!" The buck reacted by raising his head and glaring at us. I snapped a picture. This was fun. I said, "Do that again, Charlie, and I'll get another photo."

The mulie just stood there and appeared to be all in, once again dropping his head low. Charlie raised the ax and pointed it at his face again. At this, the deer lifted his head and I took another snapshot. Then the buck had had enough. He lowered his head into a challenging stance like he was ready to charge a foe. Uh oh!

Charlie said, "Surely he's not seeing us as the enemy. After all, we were standing beside him and let him go and backed off to let him have more space!"

We backed up a couple of more steps and naturally assumed the buck would be more comfortable, right? Wrong! But then maybe I was guilty of assigning human thinking and I.Q. to a deer. This was a wild animal and a mature wild buck in rut. During rut, wild animals, not unlike people, can do some strange things. We didn't know we were still inside the comfort zone of this particular deer.

Most mammals, humans included, have a comfort zone. It is like an invisible bubble that encircles us, and when someone or something gets too close or gets inside our space bubble, we become uncomfortable.

The buck came out of a submissive attitude and became hostile.

I knew a fella who was six-foot-four or -five and always stood over my six-foot-one frame with his face about a foot from mine. I would back up thinking, *Hey, fella, you are too close.* Then he would follow me, purposefully staying inside my comfort zone. I would think, *If you don't quit moving in on me, I'm going to push you back or leave.* He never seemed to hear my thoughts or read my obvious discomfort. I never did anything about it, but I sure felt like it.

We were in a similar situation with this buck. We didn't get the hint or do a very good job of reading his body language, and I blithely took more pictures—pictures the average person never gets to take but may dream about when they see professional wildlife photography.

I was so excited to get these unique pictures. He was truly a beautiful wild creature doing what deer do in a crisis. We soon learned just what they can do when they feel cornered or threatened.

After Charlie flipped the ax head up and pointed it at the deer the second time, the buck charged—straight at Charlie. I heard the thud of the deer hitting Charlie in the stomach. Charlie landed on the seat of his pants and skidded on his backside through the snow. I yelled, "Charlie! Are you okay?" All I heard was a muffled reply and some grunts.

The buck had hit Charlie square, but fortunately the buck's 30- to 35-inch wide antlers were far enough apart to go safely on each side of Charlie. A shot of adrenalin went through me, and quick as a cat I ran and grabbed the buck's antlers with both hands and began to pull the buck off Charlie.

I was straddling Charlie and face to face with the angry buck. The buck was shaking his head and trying to get loose. I was sure he would gore us if he could. I held on for dear life while Charlie tried to liberate himself. Charlie was having a struggle getting out from under the buck, along with being wedged between my legs. He finally wiggled free and stood up, apparently unhurt.

He quickly grabbed the antlers on the one side of the deer, and I shifted and got a new hold with both hands hanging on to the antlers on the opposite side as Charlie.

I need to emphasize that this buck was not acting like Bambi. My previous conception of gentle yet fearful deer was being quickly altered. Unless you have seen a deer during the breeding season, you too may have trouble believing a deer was capable of this apparent prolonged rage.

I thought back to the times I had been in close contact with mule deer when I was trapping and banding them for studies of their migration patterns in southern Utah and in Middle Park, Colorado. The hundreds of deer we trapped had wanted to escape when set free from the trap. Invariably, they would try to get away from any human and seek the safety of the natural environment.

However, I have seen the angry side of bucks before in close-up encounters with deer in captivity or before they were let out of a trap. When I was a conservation officer with the Utah Fish and Game Department, I live-trapped deer near Cedar City, Utah, in order to learn more about their summer and winter range migration routes. A few years later in my career I helped live-trap over 800 hundred deer to delineate their migration patterns in Middle Park, Colorado.

Trapping experiences verified that deer can and will be aggressive when humans are too close to the trap. Animal behavior changes when an animal is trapped and helpless. I have seen big bucks in a trap struggle to get out when a man approached the live trap. As the trap operator got close big bucks would often charge the net trying to gore the offender. In my experience, however, when a wild deer, including big bucks, was turned loose from a trap, they would invariably run hard to get away from anything human.

In our trapping operations, because of this aggressive behavior, when we captured a big buck with antlers, the first thing we did was to cut the antlers off for our own safety. (They grew new ones every year, so this was not detrimental to them.)

I have been standing outside a trap and a big buck inside would glare at me and charge into the net. Without a doubt, if he could have, he would have taken me on. Our traps were made of 4 x 4 x 8-foot pipe frames enclosed in a heavy net made of nylon cord. In the past, when these aggressive bucks were set free, they would run from us and never tried to charge.

This deer was not trapped anymore by the other buck's antlers but had not run away when given the chance. His every action indicated he was not afraid. He was snorting and breathing hard. All his instincts were on red alert. He kept trying to jerk his head free from our grasp. We were puzzled as to what to do.

Watching the buck's actions gave me a healthy respect for his moxie. He could easily have turned and gone free once he had been released by us. Normally, deer are terrified of humans.

Charlie and I had been only a few feet away when we first freed him. There were two of us to his one, yet the deer didn't seem to care. It was becoming painfully obvious that he was determined to do us in and was not interested in escape.

I didn't equate my prior knowledge of the behavior of trapped big bucks with our situation since this deer was in the open and all he needed to do was turn and bound away. We both expected the buck to do just that.

We were both getting tired of holding this buck. I said, through clenched teeth, "Let's bulldog him and get him off his feet."

Charlie looked at me and almost laughed. "Are you serious?"

I returned his look and barked, "You got a better idea?" In the meantime, the buck was pulling back, shaking his head and doing his best to free himself from our grip. But we knew instinctively that if we let him go again, he would charge one of us and that would be risky and dangerous.

Charlie shot back, "Nope!" Then he got a better hold of the antlers opposite me and grunted, "Let's do it!" We had trampled the snow cover, and the warm rays of the sun were doing their part in melting it, softening the ground and creating slippery footing in the deepening mud under the snow.

We twisted the poor buck's head until his neck was turned completely and his nose was sticking straight up into the sky. However, try as we might, we could not get him off his feet. He was too strong and too flexible, and we were handicapped by the slippery footing. In addition, we had to keep hanging on to the antlers. This made it nearly impossible to get him turned over on his side since we couldn't flank him as you would a calf.

Charlie was still manning one side and I the other. "What do we do now, Charlie? How do we get free from this devil of a buck?"

He was a big mule deer and yet he wasn't as big as a typical steer used in a bulldogging rodeo event. You'd think we could throw him down—especially since there were two of us to do the job.

Not a chance. We were both surprised that we couldn't get him down. His strength and balance combined with his agility made it impossible to get him off his feet. Perhaps if our footing was better and if we could flank him, we could accomplish the task. We thought about that, but we were unsure if one man could control him by the antlers while the other man let go in order to flank him.

What is the best solution for a couple of guys with a mature mule deer buck in their hands? They can't just drop their grip and walk away. They can't continue to just hold the buck hoping at some point he will only want to get away. This buck was mad, and his body language showed no inclination to surrender. His demeanor had changed from the time we first let him loose. Now he was so aggressive we were sure he would gore us if he could get loose.

I came up with another so-called "brilliant" suggestion. I knew Charlie would love this one. "Hey, Charlie, since we can't throw him but we can get his neck twisted with his horns pointing down, let's push his antlers deep into mud. Then maybe we can let go and run like crazy and get enough distance between us before he can get loose. Our jeep isn't that far." The truth was, we were not sure how to get away from this demon buck, and we were grasping at straws!

We decided to give it a try since we could think of no other course of action. So we pushed his antlers as deep into the mud as we could. I was almost prostrate with the effort, my chest lying across the underside of his neck, which was facing skyward. His head was twisted upside down, and his neck must have been made of rubber. He was standing with his legs all spread out and his head upside down. He was looking up at the sky and I was looking him right in the eye. It was like a cartoon.

Faces to face, we were just two men and a buck. We felt compassion in our hearts, but there was fear in our bellies. I wondered, *Are we going to be mauled? Will this work?* There was a glint of steel in the buck's eye, and I knew it would be a struggle to the end. Someone might die.

No! Stop those thoughts! We refused to admit we would not get out of this. Charlie and I knew that if it was possible, that buck was going to go free, but if it came down to who lived or who died, it was not going to be Charlie or me who died! I knew our survival demanded a winning attitude that shouts, "I will win and I will live!"

We had him pinned down, but we were breathing hard and wearing out. We rested a moment, keeping the pressure on the antlers so they would remain buried deep in the mud. We wanted to be fully ready to make a dash for it when we let go of his antlers.

We had no clue whether the mud would slow the deer down and keep him at bay, but right then we were stumped on any other way to get free from that ornery ol' buck. I said, "Charlie, this stag is like our shadow. He's like glue, and we just can't get rid of him." We knew we didn't have a good plan.

Charlie looked over at me and said, "Yup, but you better be ready, 'cause I'm going to turn loose and run like wildfire. So on the count of three, let's go. Are you ready?"

I nodded tentatively and answered, "Yeah," without much conviction.

I looked at Charlie, sighed, and loudly began counting, "1 ... and 2 ... and ..." To my dismay, before I belted out number 3, Charlie had released his grip and was scrambling toward the Jeep. I let go also. I thought I was fast, but I wasn't fast enough! I took off, but I hadn't taken three steps when, Bam! The buck rammed me square in the middle of my back with his antlers safely missing me and circling my body like they had when he'd charged Charlie.

I went to my knees. Then I lost my balance, and I found myself acting the part of a snowplow with my face and chest buried in the quagmire. I probably was one funny looking dude.

One consolation was that we were a bit closer to the Jeep. However, for the life of me, I could not decide if I was getting closer to the Jeep or closer to the grave.

It's odd what you remember and notice at moments like that. I smelled the pungent odor of the buck in full rut. This was a strong odor produced by the buck urinating all over his belly and front legs while his metatarsal glands oozed a waxy, foul-smelling, musky substance. However, knowing what this buck was capable of, I turned my attention away from such thoughts. I knew full well that this ol' codger had killed the other buck and was committed to doing the same to us.

The real issue was that he was mad and out of control. We were the object of his anger. He wanted to gore us.

I was on my belly in the muck, my hands reaching backwards holding on to his antlers like they were wheel barrow handles. I was afraid to let go because the buck might rear back and slam me with his horns. The buck had me pinned so I couldn't get my feet under me either. It didn't seem too far-fetched to think this could turn out badly and I might not see the welcome sight of home again.

We realized that we had recklessly gotten ourselves into a good deal of trouble by acting before we thought out just how to go about setting this alpha deer free. Now we were reacting instead of assertively taking action.

We had no choice, though, but to double our efforts to get control of the buck. I knew that if Charlie and I were unable to escape it could be fatal. I thought Charlie felt the same way.

Charlie was courageous and had jumped to my aid when he turned and saw that the deer had pinned me. He had gotten hold of the buck's antlers to my right and held the buck down.

I let go of that side and spun around on the ground. I switched both hands to the antlers on the buck's left but was still in the mud and snow. I looked up at Charlie and could see beads of sweat on his brow. With Charlie holding on, I managed to slide forward and onto my knees. Then, with another maximum effort, I twisted and stood up, still hanging on tightly to the antlers.

It's strange how your mind works in overdrive at times of crisis. My instinct for survival had kicked in, and I had a flashback of another night when I was faced with a desperate conflict and the need to survive was preeminent. It was a do-or-die situation.

It was a cold winter night in December when Betty, my wife, and I were in college. She worked as a waitress, and I was the cook in a small steakhouse. I was busy cooking steaks that night when I heard a commotion. Betty was doing her best to get away from a couple of drunken men who were getting out of hand and coming on to her. One of them grabbed her arm and laughed at her show of fear. Okay, now that raised my dander a notch or two—maybe 20. I left those steaks sizzling on the grill, and without the slightest thought about what I was doing, I injected myself right into the middle of the scene.

Facing the men, and with my back to Betty, I growled in an ugly voice, "You boys have to go. If you choose not to, you're going to get this steak fork right in your pretty faces."

I was trembling from a major adrenalin rush and didn't know where all this bravado was coming from, but it was there lying latent, buried deep in my soul, allowing me to have the needed strength to protect Betty.

Yes, I was going to protect that bride of mine. I believe this primal instinct exists in all males. When I see in my memory those drunks making a play for my sweetheart, I get the urge to go after them again. I still get furious when I think about them.

The two inebriates sobered up a bit and one of them said, "Yeah, we'll go, all right, but we'll be back. We're going to kick your rear and take you out."

I yelled right in his face, "You don't scare me a bit! Now get out right now or I'll call the police!"

They left, and I felt pretty weak at the knees. It was stress similar to what I was currently experiencing with the buck and our fight for our lives. A shot of adrenalin from your adrenal glands makes you feel weak at first, but once you are into the conflict, you no longer feel weak; rather, you feel empowered. That was exactly what happened to me.

Betty and I finished that night of cooking and closing up duties. It was about 1:30 in the morning when I looked out the restaurant window and saw the two souses drive up beside our car. Now, I should have been smart and called the police, but I did not. Again adrenalin did its job for me.

I told Betty I was going to go out there and take them on. I was thoroughly ticked off. My teeth were clenched and I was looking out of slits for my eyes. Betty pleaded, "No, don't go, you'll get hurt. Please stay."

Stubborn I am. Whether the issue was right or wrong, there was no turning back for me. Before Betty could protest more I was out the door. I rounded the corner from the back of the steakhouse and saw a 2 x 4 lying next to the building. I picked it up and charged right at their car. They had the motor running, and the window was down on the driver's side.

You can imagine the scene. Two drunks in a car trying to act big and tough and a young slim, almost skinny, steak cook with a 2 x 4 cocked over his shoulder daring them to get out of their car—and secretly wishing they would.

Holding the bat over my shoulder, and in the most steady and firm voice I could muster, I said with a sneer, "Go ahead and get out. I don't play fair, and I'm going to knock your heads off!" I was ready to bat like I was Babe Ruth himself. I was going to hit a home run or die trying. I think I convinced them I was no one to contend with. They must have believed me because they threw their car into reverse and laid rubber in the parking lot in their haste to flee. I stubbornly saw this insurrection to the end.

Stubbornness can get a person into trouble, but my being stubborn or obstinate in North Park was working for me just as it did at the restaurant. It occurred to me that sometimes this can be a life-saving trait.

Now here I was with Charlie and this buck deer. It was just like those many years ago at the Charcoal Broiler. We were going to finish this tussle with this old buck even if he was on the rampage. I was going to hit a home run. It would take teamwork and our combined effort, but I knew we would succeed.

We had no other ideas, so we did the same trick of sticking the deer's horns into the mud. We had noticed he was getting tired too. We would count to three, let go of the horns, and dash off toward the Jeep, knowing one of us would get hit.

We knew that the deer would charge us, but we also had learned that his horns were wide enough that they would miss us and we would only be hit by the deer's head. To further protect ourselves, when we knew we were going to get hit we would turn toward the deer so that we could grab the horns. It was easier to get up, we didn't get hit as hard, and once the person not hit came to assist we began the process again.

Using this strategy and making a run for the Jeep brought us closer to the safety of the vehicle each time we tried it. Since this seemed to be working, we kept at it again and again and took multiple hits in the process.

The buck tired and at times would let us drag him toward the Jeep, covering valuable ground safely. We would drag him when we could until he balked. Sometimes he would balk fiercely, and we'd be stuck until we could get him off balance. He would take a step or two and then he wouldn't budge at all. We would work his horns into the mud again and make another dash for the Jeep.

Each time we repeated the cycle we were closer to safety. We gained confidence and didn't feel so fearful. In fact, it was almost like a game. Mighty chancy, to say the least, but it yielded results and we inched closer to the Jeep. We simply did not have a better way to unlock ourselves from this king of mule deer.

The original goal had been to set this "victim" deer free. The objective quickly changed when the victim became the aggressor and the two do-gooders, Charlie and I, became the victims. In fact, we knew we would be fortunate to get out of this dilemma fully intact or without injury of some sort.

It seemed the buck traded off using Charlie and then me for his pin cushion. We each were charged three or four times in alternating order and usually found ourselves in the snow after each charge. We learned how to help each other and minimize the impact of each hit and how to get up when we were knocked down, valuable lessons to learn.

At last we were close to the Jeep and physically all in. Again using the "hold on to the antlers and count to three" routine, we let go and scrambled up on top of the hood. I will never forget seeing Charlie pulling himself up on the hood and "King Buck" prodding him in the rear with his antlers. We both needed a good laugh at that point.

We had fought and worked our way for at least 50 yards through mud and snow in sagebrush. We even crossed a small ravine to get to the sanctuary of the Jeep.

I still had the camera strapped around my neck, so I took more pictures. Even after all the exhausting confrontations the buck had gone through, he was still one angry buck. He glared at us on the hood, and his eyes truly seemed to be on fire, making him appear much madder than what seemed reasonable, considering the natural response most animals have toward humans.

And it wasn't over! To our amazement, the buck charged the Jeep. Bam! He hit the grill fiercely. We were flabbergasted. And worse yet, this mule deer buck now had his antlers caught in the grill of the Jeep!

It was Incredible and unbelievable. If we had not been eye witnesses, we would not have believed it. What now? Wearily and carefully, we slid down from the hood, one on each side. We warily approached the buck to free him once again. How crazy this was! I thought, *You old reprobate, I ought to be hanging your antlers over my fireplace instead of giving you freedom. Can you not figure it out? We just saved your life!*

Finally, we got on top of the jeep.

The Jeep grill held him tight. One antler tine was securely caught between the license plate and the bumper. Working as a team, I held the plate back so it would not continue to bind the deer antler point, and Charlie pulled the buck loose.

We looked at each other, grinned stupidly, counted to three again, and then let go and scrambled back up onto the Jeep hood. We made it without incident and just sat there wondering what this idiot deer would do next. The old boy stood there glaring at us as if he didn't know either. Was he finally done? Would he charge again?

Then something seemed to click with him. He gave one last look at us and turned to go, head held high. He walked off stiff-legged. Then in a bouncing mule-deer gait, he bounded away.

We had certainly had enough! He apparently had enough! He was a proud deer and never gave up. We hadn't either. We gathered up our equipment and left much wiser, understanding exactly how tough that old buck was.

The buck returned to the wild. We never saw him again, but when we saw deer peacefully browsing in the winter sun, we could envision that he was out there somewhere carrying on the function of a mature buck in the ecology of the deer herd. I bet no one took his harem for a long time.

A yearling browsing in the winter sunshine

At first we were awed by the way the events turned out. Amazingly, we were not seriously hurt. I looked at my ribs and saw a scratch on my side where an antler point penetrated my down coat and shirt. It did not break my skin and only slightly bruised me.

Wow, that was more dangerous than I thought. Charlie looked at me and I looked at him. We were stunned, speechless but ecstatic to be safe and finished with our ordeal. It was over. Strangely, in some ways we felt empty. How could we ever top this?

Now the air had gone out of the bag. We were safe, and for the first time we realized we could or perhaps we should have been severely injured.

We were overwhelmed by the way this turned out, and I could see it was not just about me, but Charlie had also been in a struggle for survival. We had been partners in our fight for life. We had triumphed and were overcomers.

We had been associates before the event, and now we were permanently bonded friends and knew we could depend on each other. It is most difficult to describe the kinship of two men who experience and survive such a trauma together.

We drove back to Walden, each of us lost in our thoughts. At the office we nodded wordlessly and went our separate ways. Charlie went home to his family, and I went to the Longhorn Café and then to the motel. I wasn't scheduled to go home until the next day. In the silence of the room I penned a poem, "The Saga of Life." This poem expressed something deep within me, and I share it as follows.

The Saga of Life
By Larry Roper

Death lurks nearby,
The patient coyotes wait,
Eagles tarry at eternity's gate.
But the victor refuses to die.

A mighty charge! Fate has its way.
Another effort, antlers locked to stay.
Two days and two nights
'Twas a blood stained fight.

A new foe,
Another blow,
The new friend is down,
But refuses to give up.

The table is turned;
Freedom is earned,
The monarch turned to go!
Will he ever know?

Pine Ridge—one could get lost here and never found . . .

Fall Colors

Chapter 2

Lost My Sweetheart on Pine Ridge

It was Saturday and a fine Indian summer day, even though it was early November. There was a hint of rain forecast for the days ahead, but today was a day to enjoy.

Everett, a friend from church, asked me to go hunting with him on his farm where good numbers of elk and deer could be found. His farm had a few acres of wheat in a lower area surrounded by a large ponderosa pine forest. This provided adequate cover and feeding areas with a creek in the bottom for water.

It was1968 and a hunter could buy both an elk and a deer tag, enabling them to hunt for either species at the same time. I took advantage of this regulation and was really happy to be able to hunt both deer and elk concurrently.

Betty was home with the kids, and I was intent on getting us some meat for the coming school year. It was the first year of my Master of Science program at the University of Idaho.

Everett and I were trying to push deer or elk to each other as we had been hunting on parallel routes. He was below me and we were at least a mile away from our rendezvous spot.

Our technique was to walk slowly a few steps, stop, and listen, dissecting every nook and cranny before we took a few more steps.

I paused and all my senses were tuned in to the terrain below. It was a likely spot for big game. A flicker of movement drew my attention to a spot on the trail about 75 yards below. There, it moved again! Now I could make out an antler. Yes, there it was.

I took another careful step. It was a white-tail buck, and judging by the antler size it was probably a three- or four-year-old. A strange excitement stirred deep within me, for I had never had the opportunity to hunt white-tailed deer. I had taken many mule deer, but a white-tail would be a real plus for me.

In this period of our life, with me as a graduate student supporting a wife and three children, this white-tail was

23

important. In fact, I would have been glad to get any deer. But this one had value as high quality food for us and it had intrinsic trophy value to me as a hunter.

Our income was from a National Science Foundation Grant plus Betty's secretarial wage. I set those thoughts aside and took careful aim. The buck dropped and I silently rejoiced. Wild grown venison doesn't have all the additives of growth hormones or any other biologic engineering.

After field dressing the deer, I crossed the draw to my left and climbed to a better trail that descended to the edge of the wheat field where we had left our pickups. Everett and I were going to meet and sit together on a stand where we could watch the winter wheat field for deer and elk to start feeding, as was their habit just before dark.

Everett was waiting for me. He had not seen any elk, although he heard my shot so he was glad to learn I had bagged a deer. Since it was nearly dark, I decided I would come back the next day to pack it out.

I told Everett, "Betty would probably like to come with me." He thought that was good as his entire family liked to hunt also. It was amazing how our ethics and family mores were so similar. He was a perfect hunting partner, even though he was about 10 years older.

The next afternoon Betty dressed in warm, rugged outdoor clothing, and we drove to the farm. The trail to the deer was a good one. We climbed to a position opposite the draw where I had bagged the buck. We were abou t a mile from the vehicles, and since we had most of the afternoon before us, we wanted to hunt awhile then pack the deer out.

I said to Betty, "We're in a good spot for deer or elk to use one of these trails below us. I'll go up this ridge and cut over

24

through the draw to the ridge where I left my deer. Then I'll cross back over to this spot, so you stay here and watch for game. I'll be back within the hour for you."

Betty said, "No, I do not really want to be left alone!"

I assured her she would be okay. I kissed her good-bye and began the climb up the ridge.

I think Betty knew me and my propensity for losing track of time when I was on a hunt. However, I had every intention of doing exactly as I said.

Climbing the ridge, I came across fresh elk sign. I followed the tracks slowly and cautiously and used my best hunting skills. I was sure I would see an elk any time. The cover had changed from an open forest to a thick, swampy western red cedar habitat that was perfect for elk to bed. I lost track of time, I was so intent on my quest.

When I finally looked at my watch I realized I would be too late getting back to Betty. I started back and noticed that the terrain didn't appear to be the same.

Apparently, I had crossed over the ridge and was going down the other side without knowing it. Betty and I were now separated by the topography, and it would be after dark before I got back to her. She was essentially lost to me as I wasn't exactly sure of where I was. Judging by the vegetation change, I was on the north side of the mountain ridge.

Meanwhile, Betty sat waiting for me and began to think about her predicament. *Boy, when I get out of here I'm going to give Larry a piece of my mind!* Tears of hot anger rolled down her face. *He's going to wish he had never married me. He is the most selfish, bull-headed man I have ever known!*

That's when Betty realized she might not get out. She was LOST. She wished she knew directions better. She was so dependent on me that she had not paid attention to how to return to the parking area.

On the other side of the main pine ridge, I could not keep my thoughts from rolling through my head. I knew I was a long way from where we'd parked the pickup. I tried to decide how to get back to the spot where Betty was sitting on her stand waiting for my return.

Under my breath I muttered, "Darn, this will cause a problem! Shoot the luck! Betty will be getting worried and scared." And I thought, *Roper, you idiot, how could you do this to her? You have got to be more aware of the time.*

My route eventually brought me to the bottom farmland several miles from Betty on the opposite side of the main ridge. It was getting late and soon would be dark. There was a farm road at the bottom of the ridge which circled around to where we'd left the vehicle.

I had a choice to make. I could stay on the road and go back to the farmland on the side where Betty was, or I could backtrack and hope I could get to her before full darkness descended upon us. To compound the problem, the sky had become heavily overcast, which would make it difficult to see well enough to find Betty or my way back to the vehicle once full night set in.

It had begun to rain lightly, and I was really getting worried and scared for Betty's safety. I believed she would stay where she was, but if she moved and tried to find me, I knew she would get lost for sure. The trail into the area was just one of many game trails and was easy hiking but not well defined. She was challenged regarding knowing her directions. Her handicap was severe and debilitating.

I thought to myself, *I better dig out my topographic map and see if I can figure out what I did and what I need to do to correct my route of travel.* The map showed me how I had crossed over the low ridge, all right, and gotten on the opposite side. Without landmarks it had been an easy mistake to make.

After I studied the map I decided to go on the road, circle around to the pickup, get a flashlight, and climb back to where I'd left her. I was in good physical shape and thought this would be the quickest way to her, since I could maintain a steady, fast pace.

This was a new experience for me, to hunt in dense, rolling terrain where a compass was so necessary. In the Colorado Rockies landmarks were usually visible, and a compass was not really a necessity like it was here in northern Idaho.

Going around the ridge took a lot longer than I thought it would. But if I had gone back through the woods I would have had a difficult time finding Betty before nightfall.

Feeling empty and hollow inside, I prayed, *Oh, Lord, keep her safe and show me the way to her. How could I have been so negligent? Is she going to be all right?*

Betty was on one side of the mountain about three miles above the meadow where we parked, and I was on the other side from Betty and the pickup. We were both praying for each other, assuming the worst case scenario for the other.

This part of Idaho was big timber country, and the hills were rolling, homogenous, pine covered ridges that had few landmarks to help guide the way. A good compass was important, and, as luck would have it, I had left mine either in the pickup or at home. I did have a good topographic map with me, however. Betty, though, had only me to rely upon, and I wasn't with her.

Betty was shivering in the light misty rain that had settled over the dense Pine Ridge forest land. She clenched her fists and then tried to relax for the umpteenth time. *What could have happened to Larry?*

Her mind was spinning, her thoughts going in circles. *He should have been back by now if he wasn't hurt. Lord, keep him safe and show me how to get out of here. I cannot get out tonight. It's too dark and I have no idea of which way to go. Maybe in the morning I can figure it out if morning will ever come.* Larry had warned her to stay where she was until he returned.

She had stayed and now it was too dark for her to work her way back to the vehicles. She began to sob softly and just wanted to curl up in a ball to forget she was ever here in this godforsaken land. Then her thoughts changed direction. She yelled, "Larry! Where are you? Oh! You make me so angry! How could you do this to me?"

Once again her mind was taken over with fear for me. She prayed out loud, "Where is he? Maybe he's dead! What could have happened? He's usually so competent. Oh, Lord, give Larry safety. Did he have an accident, or is he being his typical self and forgot about the time and, worst of all, forgot about me? Did he get lost?"

She had a nagging sense that something was wrong, and it continued to dominate her thinking. After a while she was convinced something terrible had happened.

Her thinking took several directions and her emotions vacillated wildly. She went from anger to near rage and then fear for me. As it grew colder, she shivered and her lips began to turn blue. She prayed, then she sang. She repeated this cycle over and over. She screamed, "Where are you?" There was only silence and no answer for Betty on this night.

She knew we were in prime bear country, and she became fearful of becoming a bear victim.

Betty had her rifle and knew she could shoot a bear if needed, but that didn't make her feel less afraid. She'd never had to shoot under that kind of pressure. She couldn't imagine hitting or disabling a charging bear. Her thinking was governed by fear and worst case possibilities.

She'd participated in a few hunts in prior years with her rifle and had bagged a couple of deer and an antelope. Her hunts had always been highly supported by Larry. He'd always been right by her side, making sure she was calm and handling her gun safely. He'd always made sure she aimed and squeezed the trigger rather than just point the rifle and jerk. She was a good shot but questioned her ability under pressure.

She remembered she had a sandwich in her pocket and thought to herself, *What should I do with this stupid sandwich?* She knew bears had a terrific sense of smell. Her logic told her she would probably be okay, but her emotions said, *This is not good!* So she took her sandwich and threw it as far as she could. She thought any self-respecting bear would go eat the sandwich before it would her. After thinking about it again, she came to the conclusion that all she had accomplished was to throw some bear bait out in the bushes. She would be next! She could just sense a bear was out there not far from her.

Her fear was so real that she felt she would never be found. She had heard that bears take their victims away and cover them with three or four feet of dirt and brush. Then they come back to feast on the remains time after time.

Hunter success was pretty good in the area.

Most people think of the American Black Bear as the more docile and more predictable of the bear species and races. Betty had lived in or near bear habitat most of her adult life, and she knew black bears can be ferocious at times, even though they might look like cuddly teddy bears.

Betty remembered the reports of a black bear in Rocky Mountain National Park that ripped open a tent, picked up a woman in her sleeping bag, and carried her through a barbed wire fence.

She thought about her predicament some more. It occurred to her that it was all Larry's fault. He was the most self-seeking, bull-headed man she had ever known. She realized she might not get out at all.

Then her thinking took another turn. She became more rational and began to plan. She said aloud, as if someone were there, "I know what I'll do. Tomorrow I'll just go downhill until I find the road. There has to be a road someplace."

It was getting dark and starting to rain harder. She continued on her emotional roller coaster. She cycled again and again from anger to care and concern to genuine fear, and she shed many a tear.

"What was that?" She said, hearing a noise behind her. She was petrified. Probably it was only a rabbit. Imagine being in unfamiliar mountainous terrain with a rain falling on a pitch black night. If you held your hand up in front of your face, nothing could be seen.

Time seemed to slow to a near crawl. When you are in known bear country, and you hear a noise, what do you do? Well, this young mother, without knowing it, did exactly the right thing. She prayed, she believed, she stayed put, and she waited. She also chose not to panic. She resisted every fiber in her body that was crying out in a panic saying, *This is terrible! Get up and go!*

I didn't know the specifics, but I knew Betty was probably near panic and thinking the worst. I jogged then I walked. It occurred to me to count my paces, so I jogged 100 paces, then I walked 50 paces. Finally, even though I took the long way around, I found the trail where I knew Betty should be on her stand. I had made it all the way and I felt some relief.

Without a flashlight, I climbed the hill in darkness. After some time, I knew I was within a couple hundred yards of where Betty should be waiting.

Since I couldn't see to keep on the trail, I shot three rounds into the air hoping Betty would return the fire. I waited but there was no answer. I called her name again and again. Still there was no answer. Later, Betty told me she heard me shoot and she answered by yelling and shooting her rifle three times. Apparently, in the rain and light wind, I was situated so that I couldn't hear her shots.

My fears took over and I imagined the worst. I was sure she'd tried to get out and was either lost or hurt—or both. In my mind I could see her wandering lost in the forest. Then she would panic and begin to run. I could see her stumble and fall, catching her leg between a log and a rock. I could hear the snap of the bone in her leg and hear her scream in pain.

I nearly freaked out but kept my cool enough to get back to the truck and drive to the nearest farm house. I called the church where I knew Everett would be attending. Someone finally answered the phone and I asked to speak to Everett. I told the lady it was an emergency, and she got Everett on right away.

Everett said, "Hello."

Hesitating, I just said, "Everett!" For a moment I choked up and could not get a word out.

Everett could sense something was drastically wrong and did his best to calm me. "I, ah, I lost Betty up on Pine Ridge." My voice trembled as I described to him how I was just sure some terrible calamity had occurred.

He was alarmed yet tried to give me hope. "She'll be okay, Larry. She has the Lord and she's dressed warm."

"Yeah, but you don't understand. She'll panic and tear off that mountain looking for me. I know her. She'll put my safety ahead of her own. She'll take all kinds of chances she normally would not take."

Everett was like a rock. "Calm down, Larry. Get a hold of yourself. I'll get a search party and be out there as soon as possible. Let's meet where we parked the pickups the other day, okay?"

He got all the able-bodied men in the church service to volunteer to look for Betty, then called search and rescue to get professional help. The Sheriff's Department was brought in on the rescue, also. Two search and rescue bloodhounds were a part of the menagerie of men, dogs, equipment, and especially gas lanterns. Over a hundred men responded to the call for help. The plan was to have them take positions about 50 feet apart and ascend the mountain to the top of the ridge. They would all ascend at the same time, parallel to each other.

In the meantime, I would give the bloodhounds a smell of Betty's clothing and follow as they took the trail we both had climbed. Now, I had a bright gas lantern and could easily find our tracks. The dog handler wanted me to let the dogs sniff out the trail since they were both young and in training.

I was grateful for their help, and as long as they stayed on course where Betty and I had hiked, I would put up with their training program. The dogs did get off the trail a couple of times, but I brought them back to where I knew we had walked.

I was feeling pretty broken up. This was a living nightmare. I had essentially lost hope, and I was just sure some calamity had befallen Betty.

I thought, "Will I ever see Betty again?"

Everett understood how I felt and drew me aside. He said, "Larry, you believe in God and trust Him, don't you?"

I said. "Yes, I do."

Everett looked me straight in the eye, put his hands on my shoulders, and like a concerned father, gave me a shake and said, "Then trust Him for the safety of your wife."

I had let my emotions cloud my thinking. I prayed a quick prayer. It calmed me and I felt much better. Now I was able to think positive reinforcing thoughts. It was hard to describe my overall feelings at this point, but I was filled with adrenalin and yet had peace, or perhaps it was confidence. I could have run all the way up the mountain without much effort.

We were getting close to where I'd left Betty, so I gave a loud hoot. I called her name and to my great relief she yelled back in the sweetest tones I'd ever heard: "I'm over here!" I ran to her. We hugged and wept and then went back down the mountain with the men and dogs. It was in the wee hours of the morning. Betty and I were worn out, for this had been an ordeal.

After thanking the men in the search party, we drove home and discovered the church women had gathered at our house and were taking care of our children. It was a while before we finally had time to come down off our high and get some rest.

This event was hard for me to live down. In the paper the next day was a headline that said "Local Spouse Only Stayed as Ordered." The write-up was not flattering to my ego, nor was the news on the radio. Typical of small towns where they need newsworthy stories, the local radio station broadcast the tale every hour on the hour as though it was the biggest news event of the year.

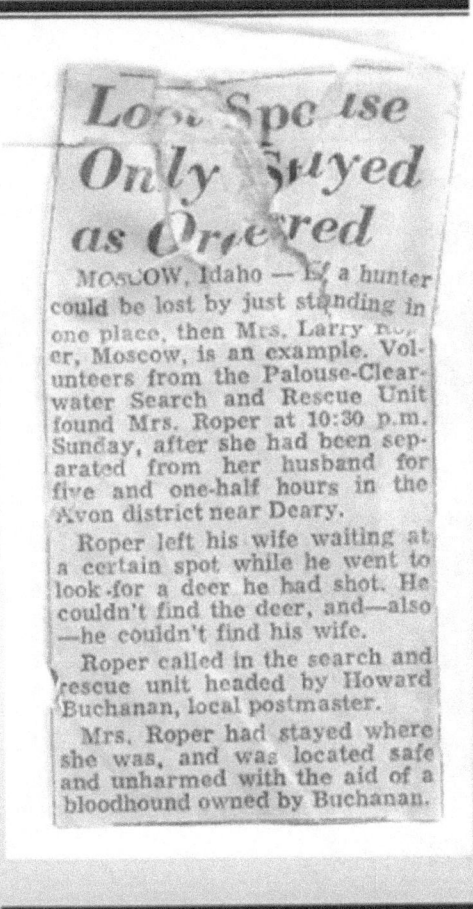

The local newspaper printed the story.

Lost Spouse Only Stayed as Ordered

MOSCOW, Idaho — that a hunter could be lost by just standing in one place, then Mrs. Larry Roper, Moscow, is an example. Volunteers from the Palouse-Clearwater Search and Rescue Unit found Mrs. Roper at 10:30 p.m. Sunday, after she had been separated from her husband for five and one-half hours in the Avon district near Deary.

Roper left his wife waiting at a certain spot while he went to look for a deer he had shot. He couldn't find the deer, and—also —he couldn't find his wife.

Roper called in the search and rescue unit headed by Howard Buchanan, local postmaster.

Mrs. Roper had stayed where she was, and was located safe and unharmed with the aid of a bloodhound owned by Buchanan.

The old self-image said, yes, I was the great white hunter and I knew no bounds. I was ready to go whenever the wilderness called. But now I was the great white loser. I could not even keep track of my sweet Betty.

The next morning, with sleep still in my eyes, I arrived at my office cubical where all the graduate students worked on their theses and studied for tests and other school related functions. "Hey, Larry, did you find your wife this morning?" I heard a lot of laughter.

Another whistle and Bob said, "Tell me how to lose my wife. Then maybe you could tell me how to find another! Ha ha!"

My face was red and I mumbled an answer. I thought, *Boy, if those guys only knew the reality of what stress we experienced. How can I ever live this thing down?*

In spite of my chagrin, I learned a great lesson or two. I learned I needed to always keep rendezvous plans and to be where I say I will be. I also learned to trust the Lord in all circumstances. It was a great blessing to see people respond to our need and to be a part of God's answer to our prayers.

The men even helped get my deer down to the pickup. I was a young and foolish man thinking I was an invincible outdoorsman, able to do just about anything in the wild country. I had a big helping of humble pie that night, and I had to eat just about all of it. Although Betty said she still loved me, she decided she would never let me leave her alone in the woods or mountains ever again, and to this day she never has.

Betty still loves me

Chapter 3

A Good Day to Die (Plane Down!)

The day was exhilarating and a balm to the soul. The sky was clear, and the azure blue was so deep it was a never ending heaven. The wind was streaming past the fuselage. I let go of the roll of toilet paper and watched it stream down towards the ground.

Suddenly, the sound changed from a normal slipping and soughing of the airstream to a screeching whistle of air racing past the fuselage skin. We were electrified by adrenalin surging through our bodies.

Fate had finally caught up with me. Time had run out. I had played my last card. This was the final adventure. I knew we were going to die! My friend Larry "Scrib" Scribner and I were hurtling pell-mell to earth in his bush plane.

We were going down onto a steep, brush covered hillside in wild Alaska. It was a rugged wilderness, and there was no hope for a safe landing, a quick rescue, or a chance to bail out. This was it!

I could just see Betty in her grief looking at me lying so still in a casket. She would probably say, "You took too many chances, and I knew it would end this way. What am I going to do now? I guess I'll just have a big potlatch funeral for you." A potlatch is a three- or four-day ceremony practiced by the native Indian populations of the north. Since we were missionaries to the Ahtna Indians of the Copper River Valley, Betty would think a potlatch funeral would be in order. It is a celebration of the life of the deceased and a time of giving gifts to help the relatives grieve.

We were sinking fast toward our demise! Although we were hurtling to the earth, it felt more like the earth was coming at us like a charging grizzly.

Scrib cried out, "We're going down!"

"I know!" I yelled.

We didn't have much time, but Scrib was doing his best to prepare for a crash. He shut the gas off then concentrated on

35

keeping us from going into a spin, as is often the case with a stalled plane.

A miraculous peace came over me that can only be explained as the peace the Lord gives. This was not a chance event where we might beat the odds and be able to brag about it. The only way we could live to tell about this experience would be through the working of a miracle.

It was one of those idyllic, warm Indian summer days, and even though there was a need to do everything at once, I'd felt lazy in the warm fall sun, like lying on the bank of the river and watching the clouds float by. I'd yearned to get out into the mountains and wander through the wild country, and it had been an easy decision to help my friend Scrib.

I climbed aboard Scrib's plane, reveling in the beauty of the day. Like me, Scrib was an avid hunter, trapper, and fisherman. He was also a high school Social Studies and English teacher. We had flown together several times and had learned to trust each other's outdoor skills. We did not know it at the time, but this trust did not come without a price. We would be tested and have to endure hardship and calamity to seal our bond of trust.

We were headed for a remote area in the Wrangell Mountains, to an airstrip that was nothing more than a brushed out gravel bar alongside the river. It was maintained on a somewhat regular basis by the few bush pilots who used the area. It was all of 300 feet long and required skill to take off and land, especially in inclement weather with various loads of big game trophies, meat, and camping gear. We called it the Cheteslena strip, as did most of the locals who knew about it.

Every takeoff and landing required accepting high risk, which could not be ignored if a person was going to successfully fly in the bush. Bush planes are specially equipped with stall wing tips, balloon tires, and souped-up motors. They represent the backbone of transportation in rural Alaska. In fact, without bush planes and pilots, Alaska would not be what Alaska is today. They were and are as important to the development of rural Alaska as the horse was to the development of the West.

Scrib knew I had not been caribou hunting yet. Caribou are important subsistence animals in the far north. We depended on them as a source of protein. We turned the meat into quality sausage, hamburger, steaks, and roasts. Much of the scrap cuts went into stews. A delicious stew can be made using typical garden vegetables that grow voraciously in the long summer days of the north.

Scrib knew I liked to get a caribou and a sheep before moose season started. A caribou hunt would be just the ticket, since I already had my sheep. He suggested I might get a caribou while we packed his meat in to the camp.

He told me he had knocked down two bulls near Sheep Gulch, and we would first fly over them and get a fix on where they lay. He had field dressed his two bull caribou the night before he solicited my help to pack them out. He said they were about eight miles up the river from the airstrip.

We finally spotted the two caribou carcasses. Scrib circled them and then flew up the valley. He banked a turn and came back over the bulls. They lay on the steep mountainside well above the tree line in brush about waist to shoulder high.

I planned to drop a roll of toilet paper and let it stream out to mark the site so we could find it easily on the ground. Then we would fly back to the Cheteslena airstrip, land, and hike in the eight miles to the caribou.

Scrib flew slowly and had the stall flaps set. I dropped the roll out so it would provide a streamer to see. As skillful a pilot as Scrib was, he made a critical mistake. He looked back, inadvertently lifting the nose of the plane. We lost our air!

Little did we know it would take a mir   acle to bring us home. We were flying eastward toward the Cheteslena drainage between the 14,100-foot Mount Wrangell peak and the 12,900-foot Mount Drum.

I was sitting on a makeshift plywood seat with a seat belt but no shoulder harness. I held Scrib's rifle in my right hand with the butt end of the stock on the floor of the fuselage, and I held my Ruger .338 Magnum in my left hand in similar fashion.

A thousand thoughts whipped through my mind. The most significant was this great sense of God's presence. I thought, *So this is what it's like to die!* Then I remembered my family and how I wanted to see my girls and my boy grow up. I was going to miss all of their basketball games. What would Betty do without me?

We were going into the side of the mountain, nose first, but Scrib skillfully kept us from spiraling and he was able to get the nose of the plane up. Instead of drilling a hole into the earth, our airplane hit flat as a pancake into the hillside. In most light plane accidents involving a stall, planes tend to spiral and then nose-dive into the ground. In such cases, pilot and passengers have little chance of surviving.

I heard ripping metal, and then dust filtered up through the cockpit. Silence, and the realization we were both alive. I was amazed!

"Are you okay"? Scrib asked me. I looked around.

"Yeah, I think so. Are you?"

"I think I'm all right," he replied as he crawled out of the plane.

I tried to lift my leg over the front seat, but when I got about halfway, I felt an excruciating pain in the middle of my back. This pain would not subside until much later, after I got medical aid.

Outside the plane, Scrib walked around it and kept repeating, "Oh, Lord, I've done it now! I have done it now!" He appeared disoriented and very upset. The left wing was severed from the fuselage and the landing gears were smashed up against the body of the plane. The left plexiglass window was broken with jagged pieces sticking out at odd angles.

Just under my chin I pulled out a piece of the plexiglass, causing some bleeding in a wound in my throat. Later the doctor showed me it was next to my jugular vein, and then he pulled out another small piece before he stitched the wound. I thought, *Wow, a crash like that and I was nearly killed by a piece of plastic rather than a body maiming, twisted piece of cold, unforgiving metal.*

I handed Scrib his rifle and then mine. As I gave him my Ruger, it broke into two pieces at the trigger guard. Now I was without a working firearm. This seemed like a big loss to me until I compared it to the fact that neither of us had lost our lives.

I handed Scrib some of our survival gear such as sleeping bags, flash light, and freeze dried food. Then, grasping the cowling above the door, I pulled myself up and was able to get my legs out and fall to the ground. I crawled away from the plane, fearing it could burst into flames.

The pain in my lower back was horrific. The seat belt had failed and was torn from its bracket. However, regardless of the appearance of the wreckage and other than a tremendously injured back, I was alive and seemed to be okay. Reality set in and we both knew this was no picnic.

Scrib was not seriously injured. I could see that he had facial cuts, and his rambling, unfocused speech indicated a severe concussion. But truly the Lord had blessed us, even though we were down for the count.

"Let's get farther away from the plane. There might be a fire," Scrib said. I already knew I had to get away, so I crawled a few more feet into a depression under the right wing and I just lay there, helpless and unable to move without sharp, unbearable pain.

Scrib was disoriented. "Where are we?" he repeatedly asked. "What are we doing here?" Even though his disorientation waned, he was still confused enough that he wanted to walk out for help. I convinced him he could not do that as it was about 30-35 miles to the nearest road, and I needed him to stay and help.

"Scrib," I said, "you need to set up a wilderness survival camp and get me into a sleeping bag. I'm going into shock, and I think the danger of the plane exploding into flames has passed."

He got me into a sleeping bag and then began to get out equipment. He opened the first aid kit and gave me some codeine pain pills. I might just as well have taken lemon drops, for all the good they did.

Scrib got three flares, the emergency locater, and some survival food. It was good to see him coming around in his thinking. He was starting to perform like the old Scrib I knew.

He set the locater on the tail wing of the plane, only to discover that the locater wasn't putting out a signal. This sobering fact made us realize no one was going to come looking for us for at least a couple of days since we weren't expected back any sooner. Our only hope was to be seen by some pilot flying over us, in which case our flares should help him see us. But we knew that was unlikely unless another hunter just happened to be checking out the area for a hunt of his own.

Scrib was exhausted by this time but was thinking more clearly. He got his sleeping bag and lay down beside me. We prayed for our families and our rescue then read from my pocket New Testament. We lay there in our lonely and desperate situation. We were just two guys in the wilderness knowing we needed help. We could see snow-capped mountain peaks and ice drips forming little icicles on the edge of the wing tip of the plane. In our hardship, we were bonding as two pals. We worked out survival strategies together.

Our next step was to doctor some of our injuries. "Scrib, your face is a mess. Here, let me put bandages on those cuts in your face." He showed me his tooth that had been knocked out. Then he put it in his pocket. "What on earth are you saving that for?" I asked.

"I don't know, maybe as a keepsake."

I laughed. "Ha! You must think we're going to get out of here!"

"Sure, is there any other way to think?"

It was midmorning and we heard a plane in the distance. "Did you hear that?" I asked. "It's a plane. Listen, it's coming closer. Sure is high. I wonder if they will be able to see us." Our hopes began to rise as it came closer. Finally we could see it high above us. In fact, it was so high it would have been useless to set off a flare.

We watched as it disappeared into the cloudless sky. I said to Scrib, "Well, that's the way it goes." We were disappointed, but we still had faith that we would see this through to a happy conclusion.

Scrib set about gathering some dead branches of brush, since there were no trees to provide a good source of firewood. Time seemed to stand still. Hours passed and the sun was just beginning to dip down near the horizon when we heard another plane coming up the valley below us.

Yes, we were sure it was coming up our drainage! Scrib got up and went to the flares to be ready to set one off. The plane was actually below us, and we could tell it was not going to come any higher. The pilot began to bank and turn to go back the way he had come.

Scrib quickly shot off a flare. "Oh, no, it's a dud!" He shot off another. "Blast, another dud!"

My stomach tightened up, I began to sweat, and my breathing rate increased. I thought to myself, *He won't see us!* Then Scrib shot the last flare, and I prayed, "Lord, we need this one to work!"

It worked! A plume of smoke shot into the air. Our elation did not last, though. "Look at that," said Scrib. "He didn't even wiggle his wings to acknowledge he saw us."

We watched as the plane just flew off and disappeared. He was following the river back toward civilization, and we felt like it was our last chance for help on that day. In my despair I said, "Yeah, that's probably the last plane we'll see until tomorrow."

Night was coming, and the clear sky sucked the remaining heat out of the air. We could tell winter was just around the corner. It was that quiet hour just before all light is lost except for the stars and moonlight, creating an eerie feeling experienced when it is just you and the elements of the wilderness.

I knew I had a severe back injury and having a good friend, one usable rifle, and some high quality survival gear made me feel I could get out and back to my family again.

The wilderness was beautiful, but it was intolerant of mistakes. To get along in the back country a man must go with the weather and the seasons. He must become part of the environment and not a visitor. If you are going to fly, then fly like the eagle and use the air currents. Glide and pay attention.

It was almost ten hours after crashing, when suddenly we heard in the far away distance the slight sound of a chop, chop, chop. It was a helicopter and it was coming up our drainage. It

42

seemed to be on a string and zoned in on us. We were almost afraid to be grateful, fearing it would not be coming for us and would pass us by. But not so; it was coming for us. I said, "Oh, thank you, Lord! He really is coming our way." The earlier plane had indeed seen us and relayed our plight!

There was no place close for the chopper to land. After circling around us, the pilot flew about 100 yards to a slight knoll below us and hovered, letting his crewman jump off. He climbed to us and helped us gather a few essentials.

The reality of our situation came as a big surge of pain hit me hard. I was being dragged between our rescuer and Scrib through the brush to the hovering aircraft.

I grabbed the struts at about chest high and pulled, and they pushed me up and aboard. The pain was terrific. Scrib crawled in next and sat beside me while the co-pilot, our rescuer, was in the front passenger seat beside the pilot.

Camp and survival gear lay scattered on the ground. We could leave it all behind. We sure didn't need that stuff now, because we were on our way!

The two men manning the chopper were from the Alyeska Oil Pipeline crew and were two men we will never forget. This rescue was like a lot of rescues by courageous men. They were just doing their job and would do it again if called upon.

I sat in excruciating pain and mercifully blacked out about half way to Glennallen. Scrib held my head in an upright position, although I was not aware of it. The next thing I remember was a lady nurse taking charge and not letting them move me until I was safely tied down on a backboard with my head strapped tight and immovable. I heard her say, "Don't you dare move him until I get him stabilized." *Hm, she must think I'm really injured.* Then I felt a sharp pain. *Maybe she's right. Maybe my back is serious.*

Soon we were transported to Faith Hospital, a small emergency medical center supported by Send of Alaska Missions. The doctors, nurses, and support staff are all missionaries serving in their field of expertise.

X-rays told the doctors that I had crushed vertebrae but should recover just fine. Scrib had a concussion, facial cuts, and a hole where a tooth used to be. The doctor took Scrib's tooth, which he had put in his pocket at the time of the crash, washed it, and put it back in the hole. To our surprise, that tooth continued to stay alive, and other than some pain and looseness at first, Scrib discovered it truly healed.

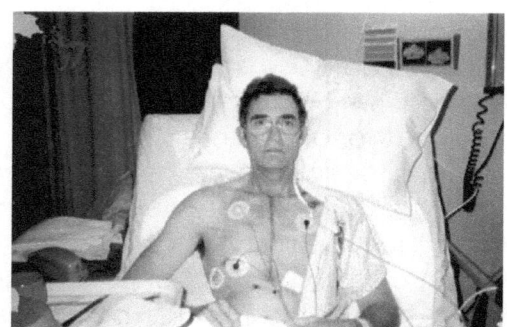

Larry got checked out at Crossroads Emergency Medical Clinic.

The ensuing events and activities in the hospital were a blur to me. I remember my family being there, but details escape me. I was just glad to be in the ER and glad to receive some expert attention from the medical staff. I was not left alone, as our native friends visited nearly around the clock and someone was sitting with me most of the time. I was aware that many came and went.

That airplane crash was in 1981, and now nearly three decades later the memory of that beautiful September day in Alaska is still clearly etched in my mind. Through the years I have often thought of the lessons I learned in our traumatic plane crash in the remote Wrangell Mountains. I believe one of the significant changes was to make me more mellow, patient, and forgiving when things go wrong.

When I remember that day, the first image that comes to me is the change in sound and the change of flight pattern the moment we lost our air cushion. That was the moment we lost control and began our rapid descent. Our lives are like that. As long as we think we have some control, we cope with whatever happens pretty well, but when we lose control of our circumstances that is the time our character is tested. That is the true test of our mettle. The question is, can we pass the examination?

Betty and I now live in rural Nebraska near Scottsbluff. I have semi-retired from a Christian counseling ministry. Both Scrib (Larry Scribner) and I know God has been good to us and has given us fruitful years beyond what was a near fatality. I believe that crash was a pivotal moment in my life. And God used it to move me on to a deeper relationship of trust with Him.

"I will walk and I will pack again. I will return to the Cheteslena."

Mr. Weasel, king of the cabin

Chapter 4

A Weasel Joins the Family

The air was crisp and the sky a clear blue. I had wanted to take Betty and our kids Lori and Laren on a good hunt for caribou and sheep before I got honed in on getting a moose. When moose hunting season opened the first day of September, all my hunting of other game took a back seat.

It was the last week of August, and we planned to hunt caribou and Dall sheep north of the Dadina River cabin in a drainage that headed on Mt. Drum. Lori was 15 years old and Laren was 14. Our friend Larry Scribner (Scrib) was flying us in to the cabin.

Lori and Betty explore around the cabin.

The cabin would serve as our base camp. We would stay up to four days. Kristi, our oldest daughter, was married and living in Fairbanks. We wished she could have been with us, as the setting was perfect for us as a family.

The cabin had nostalgia and aesthetics to the limit. I bet if that cabin could talk, it would say, "Oh, boy, am I glad a couple of women are here with these two hunter guys. Now I can expect to get a good cleaning, and I sure need it!"

We explored and cut firewood to last a few days. We had to wait until morning to hunt. That way we would have an early start, and we would be in compliance with Alaska's no hunting on the same day you fly rule.

Lori wanted to make biscuits. We already had an open fire going outside the cabin and I had a reflector oven. So Lori took over the culinary duties and fixed us biscuits. They turned out great, and loaded with melted butter and plenty of jam, they were fit for a king! My mouth is watering right now just thinking about them.

Around bedtime we heard a rustling in the corner of the cabin. Soon Mr. Weasel showed up as if to say, "Hey, what did you guys do to my home?"

We soon realized he was in his home and was the one being invaded. Mr. Weasel was wearing his brown coat with whitish-yellow trim on his underbelly. But as fall progressed into winter, his coat would change to pure white, except for a black tip on his tail. When arrayed in a white coat, weasels are known as ermines.

Weasels are mighty and courageous little predators, as are their cousins. All of the Mustelidae family have strong smelling musk glands and emit a powerful odor when aroused.

This little guy's fearlessness and presence in the cabin was something for us to look forward to at night. The kids especially enjoyed watching him scurry about the cabin. He would disappear behind some of our gear only to appear somewhere else. What fun to try to guess where he would pop up next. For us, the folk song "Pop Goes the Weasel" took on new meaning!

The weasel has a slender, long body similar to mink and marten. In contrast, the short, squat, bow-legged members of these musky carnivores are the badger and wolverine.

The kids were curious about the weasel, so I took the opportunity to teach them about the weasel family. I told them that the critters making up the weasel family are skunks, mink, marten, otter, fishers, Russian sables (found in Europe and Asia), badgers, and wolverine. All are fierce and courageous and fit into unique ecological niches.

Skunks and badgers are the only representatives not found too far north. These weasel-like species prey upon small rodents, squirrels, rabbits, and snowshoe hares.

The skunk with its plume tail makes up a separate group of this family. The last group is comprised of the otters and fishers. They are aquatic and have thick tapering tails that are good rudders.

Surrounding the cabin area, the pine marten made his abode. The marten was a hunter of squirrels. In fact, they only live in habitat where squirrels abound.

I told the family about how one winter I watched a squirrel sitting on a limb after a fresh snow. A quiet hush covered the cold winter landscape. A pine marten was quietly resting, relaxed yet ready to pounce at any moment. The pine squirrel began to chatter nervously from his lofty perch high in the lodgepole pine. The branches of the tree were covered with at least an inch of fresh snow.

An explosion of frosty snow filled the air as the marten sprang into action with a flash of movement. Even as quick as squirrels are, they are no match for the pine marten.

The weasel at the cabin was as quick as the marten, yet not as secretive. He made himself known to us and let us understand in the best way he knew how that he was king. His behavior showed us that he was the major mouse hunter of the cabin.

Sleep finally came to us and morning was soon upon us. After a hearty breakfast we packed our day packs and started up the river to the best place to ford the river.

It was our second day at the Dadina River cabin. We had eaten breakfast, packed our day packs, and left the cabin in high spirits.

About 200 yards up the river from the cabin, we needed to cross the swift glacier-fed Dadina River. I had the only pair of hip boots. The plan was for me to take the packs across first and then let Laren, Lori, and Betty ride piggyback. The water was swift and just above my knees. The bottom was shale rocks about six to eight inches in diameter and slick.

I needed a good stout stick to help me resist the current and maintain balance. I found a dry cottonwood about three inches in diameter and about six feet long. It appeared strong enough to do the job.

First, I took our day packs and rifles across and then the kids. I turned to Betty and jokingly said, "It's your turn."

In jest she replied, "It looks too dangerous to me. I think I'll stay here and play with the grizzlies."

"Well, okay," I said, "the kids and I will go hunting and we won't be back till after dark."

She quickly thought about it and said, "All joking aside, I am ready to take the risk and ride across."

I stepped into the river with Betty perched on my back. I wavered while I was trying to maintain balance using the staff.

Crack! It broke! I was leaning so hard on the pole that I lurched forward, hurling Betty over my head.

Betty's teeth were chattering. Her lips were blue. "Oh! Brr, this is cold." She said. "If I could, I'd push you in head first and see how you like it!"

The kids and I were laughing, and finally Betty saw the humor in the situation and began to laugh with us. She had gone in head first into the icy glacial stream. It was so cold it would even make a grown man cry.

I quickly tried to grab her and stumbled. I sloshed around, slipping with each attempt to stay upright, and nearly fell. I couldn't react quickly enough to save Betty from a complete bath. The river was so swift and cold, she couldn't regain her balance and stand up.

"Oh, let me help you. I can't stand up either!" I stumbled and sloshed around, slipping with each attempt to stay upright.

She recovered quickly and with my help was able to stand up. I held her hand and we both made it out, even though we were slipping and sliding. We crawled out, and after more apologies, Betty good-naturedly said, "It's okay, but don't let it happen again!" We went back to the cabin and she changed clothes.

While Betty changed, I could see Lori and Laren sitting on a log where we had crossed the stream. It looked like they were still laughing. I got my ax and went into the spruce forest next to the cabin and cut a good green pole that would not break and went back to the cabin to get Betty.

The kids were still chuckling when we got back. It must have been quite a sight. We all had another good laugh and could see the genuine humor in the situation. Other than wet clothes, there was no harm done.

During our second attempt, the kids were shouting and laughing each time I took a step and nearly slipped. They were yelling, "You can make it this time, Dad! We know you can!" I was struggling to stay on my feet, leaning on the pole for balance and trying to keep from slipping. Betty, in her finest humor, leaned forward from her piggyback position and whispered in my ear, "I love you."

Boy, I almost fell again! But those three little words gave me new energy and increased my resolve not to dump her again. I made it across and we were all ready to get on with the hunt. I gave Betty that sexy knowing look we both knew and gave her a great big bear hug.

Betty and I are getting ready to fly into the Dadina River cabin. Friends Verlin and Ruth Ringle, summer missionaries, see us off.

Larry laid the hip boots on a log.

The crossing was completed and I laid the hip boots across a log to be ready for us when we returned that evening.

This was Lori's first big game hunt. We were really looking forward to this hunt. Betty set the pace, and she was considerably less driven to fill her hunting license than I was. She simply wanted a terrific family time together.

After I had dumped Betty in the river and our second attempt at getting her across was successful, we hiked northward seriously on our hunt.

We had been hiking for about an hour when we spotted a grizzly. He was high on the slope above us to the west. The bear was ambling along in a grazing mode. We watched him feed on grass and blueberries for a while, and then we continued hiking. Soon we spotted another bear. We were amazed at just how big and beautiful they were. We felt comfortable as they were a good distance from us.

We hiked up the river leaving the bears behind grazing in solitude.

It wasn't long before Laren spotted a big, heavy-antlered caribou. He was on the same hillside as the bears but farther up the trail.

Laren and Betty watched where the caribou lay down while Lori and I made a sneak. We had to cross a rock slide to get to a spot where Lori could shoot.

We were focused on being extra quiet when the rocks on the steep mountain slope began to slide. "Lori, quickly jump over here and get out of those rolling rocks," I whispered.

"Wow, that was slippery!" Lori exclaimed, in as quiet a voice as she could muster.

"Shush, let's not spook that caribou!"

The caribou stood up and was broadside to us. We were

sure it had heard the rattling of the rocks. Lori sat quickly and took a careful aim. She was thrilled to see the bull drop and so was I.

Betty and Laren quickly climbed the hillside to see the trophy. Betty started sneezing and could not quit. Apparently, she was allergic to something in the area, so she and Laren decided to go down to the river and wait. The river was not far as it was no more than 150 to 200 yards away. Lori and I finished skinning the caribou. Before joining Laren and Betty for lunch, we boned the meat and got it ready to pack into four packs.

After lunch I started up the slope to pack the meat down to the main trail. Betty noticed I didn't have my rifle and said, "Honey, I think you better take your rifle. Those two grizzlies are not far away."

"Oh, I don't think I'll need it." I replied. "We've made enough noise and left plenty of human scent around so that no self-respecting bear will stay around."

Now, this was erroneous thinking on my part. But some of us must learn things the hard way, and this day would prove that point. I walked on up the hill without a rifle. The truth is, I was thinking about having my hands free to hang on to bushes as I came down such a steep slope heavily laden. I was also thinking I would preserve my strength a bit.

Betty must have thought to herself, *What a nut. He is so bullheaded! I cannot tell him a thing even if I am right. I hope if he runs into a bear and it gives him a good scare, maybe he'll learn to carry his rifle all the time in bear country.*

I climbed up to the first bench, and as fate would have it, I came face to face with a big, brown grizzly about the length of a semi truck trailer away from me. This distance is about what I consider to be the boundary of a bear's comfort zone. If a person gets any closer he is in danger. At that distance the bear might feel threatened and decide to charge. This bear just stood there in a non-threatening stance.

It seemed the bear was trying to make a decision. I had already made my decision. I believed if I turned around and went back to get my rifle, then I would be more vulnerable for an attack than if I held my ground and yelled for Laren to bring the rifle to me. Yelling would be something the bear was not used to, but he was familiar with prey that ran from him and he would give chase.

I yelled at Laren to bring a rifle. And there I stood with no gun and a grizzly between me and his possible dinner. We probably both wanted that caribou.

Of course, I had the caribou all boned and ready for a bear picnic. I turned around and yelled, "Laren! Bring the rifle!" I thought, *Boy, that sure was a dumb maneuver not bringing my rifle with me. That's why I carry a .338 WM.* I'll never go without a rifle again. I'll have to tell Betty she was right. The bear was real, and with the dead caribou not far away, the danger was imminent.

A bear in the alders is a scary proposition.

Laren thought for sure I had seen another caribou, and he eagerly climbed up to me. Breathlessly, he asked, "Where's the caribou?"

"It's not a caribou," I said. "It's a grizzly, and there he is!"

At about 15 to 20 yards from us, the bear looked as big as a mountain. As I pointed, the bear woofed dropped to all four feet, turned, and ran off. Thankfully, he had made his decision and I hoped he was happy with it, because the caribou lay among dense alders. A bear in the alders can be scary. Not just scary! It is downright dangerous.

It seemed that the bear had not taken my caribou. It was obvious he had been in route to it, following the scent. If he had already been to the sacks of meat and the carcass, he would have protected the meat and taken a defensive posture. He would have guarded the carcass, making short runs at us, woofing and clicking his teeth. When a hunter sees such bold defiance, he is wise to back away and let the bear have the meat.

With relief, we watched the bear disappear into the alders. Laren said, "We have to be careful here in this thick cover. That ol' bear might just be waiting for us. And if he is, we could be in real trouble." Cautiously, we proceeded to the kill site. Laren said, "Look, Dad, nothing has been eaten."

"Yeah, all the meat is still where we left it," I replied. "That doesn't mean he won't come back at any time, though."

We quickly got as much meat as possible to tote to the river. There was at least one more load to get. This would allow Betty and the kids a bit more rest time before we started back to the cabin. I went back up the hill for the last load and, believe me, I took my rifle. That .338 Winchester Magnum didn't seem to be too much gun at all. It was worth its weight in gold.

We now had all the boned meat moved down to the main trail alongside the river. Everyone seemed to be rested. "I'll take the lion's share of the load so you guys won't have quite so much to carry," I said.

Then Betty said, "Thanks a lot, but whatever I have to carry it will be too much!"

The kids had appropriate loads, and they were sure it was too much. Good naturedly, I said, "Complaining won't get us anywhere, so cheer up—it could get worse, and it probably will!"

We started off working our way over the gravel and rocks, which were just the right size to impede our steps and easily cause a twisted ankle. We encountered no problems and were glad for that.

We hiked about three hours and took plenty of rest stops in getting back to the cabin. Everyone was amazed that it would take three hours to go the route that only took one hour coming in. They were all glad we took our time and had plenty of rest and recuperation breaks.

"Honey, I'm getting exhausted. I don't think I can keep going," Betty said with a smile that belied how sore and tired she was.

With Betty and the kids getting exhausted and discouraged, it was no longer a fun outing in the Wrangell Mountains. Laren was trudging along, not saying much.

Somehow Laren's pack got off balance on a precarious spot in the trail, and he suddenly fell backwards off the trail, doing a somersault and landing on his feet. "Dad, it's so steep and you loaded me too heavy. I want you to reload me with less weight!" he exclaimed.

"Nice try, Son, but if I give you a lighter load then someone else will have a heavier load. We better keep it like it is and just take a good rest, but keep going and get back to camp."

We gave him a hand up and all of us had a good laugh. Betty said to Laren, "You did that somersault on purpose! How did you land on your feet? You are amazing!"

"We are acting like a bunch of sissies," I teased.

"But, Dad, I am a sissy!" Lori said.

"No, Lori, sissies don't shoot bull caribou and hike with a pack on their back for five or six miles. So you've already proved you aren't a sissy. Even though the packs are like lead weights, we still have to get them into camp. But I promise we will take it slow and rest often."

Back at the river ford, the river was more dangerous than it had been in the morning, but the trusty green pole was waiting to aid us in the crossing. The river was typical of glacier fed streams, which usually got deeper due to increased glacier melt as daytime temperatures rose. Glacial streams in Alaska are a murky gray and about 32 to 40 degrees Fahrenheit. We made the water crossing back to the cabin just fine, although I got some water inside my hip boots.

After a hearty supper and camp chores, we were entertained by Mr. Weasel. Then we all went to sleep and slept the sleep of exhaustion. Morning came all too quickly. I was up as usual bright and early. "Come on, guys, let's get up! Rise and shine ♫ ♫ and give God the glory, glory. ♫ ♫" My singing left a lot to be desired, but it achieved the objective of getting the family awake. Betty and Lori quickly decided to stay in camp. Their bodies were aching, and it was most difficult to see at 5:30 a.m.

Laren's determination to get a sheep or caribou helped him get up, eat, and get going. We left the cabin with our minds full of anticipation of a successful hunt.

Laren and I saw no game as we travelled in on the same trail we were on the day before. We were perhaps two miles above the site where Lori got her caribou and were resting before getting ready to climb Snider Peak when we spotted a couple of young bull caribou. Laren set up for a shot, but the bulls were intent on crossing the North Fork and moving on before they were within shooting range.

We watched them go. Then we decided to take a side drainage west of us into what looked like good sheep habitat on the east side of the peak. We had not gone far when we spotted two big Dall rams standing on the edge of a cliff above us. They appeared to be watching us.

I looked for a good route to get closer, but the terrain was too rough. The rams were over 300 yards away, although it was difficult to tell. Sky-lined animals usually look bigger or closer than they really are.

Nevertheless, Laren wanted to try a shot. We found a good-sized boulder for a rest, and I arranged Laren's pack on the rock so he could get as steady an aim as possible and squeeze the trigger just like he did with the previous year's caribou.

Laren followed my instructions perfectly. The shot echoed up and down the canyon, and the rams turned and ran. We hardly had time to see them go.

A clean miss!

We decided to climb up the ravine to find a way above the ledge the ram had been standing on in hopes of finding him. We began the climb. It would take us about 50 yards above the cliff.

We were making good progress and were almost to the top when we came to a shale-covered chute about 15 feet across. It was steep and if we slipped, it would certainly skin us up. We looked for a better route but could not find any other way we could finish our stalk on the sheep. I knew crossing that chute would be a dangerous maneuver but not life threatening.

After looking the chute over carefully, we decided we could make it. I went first and told Laren the secret was to run across and keep moving or we would take a big slide. I ran across and made it safely, although with some slipping and sliding. I followed my own advice and kept my feet moving.

It was Laren's turn, and I said a quick prayer.

Laren looked at me, smiled, and said, "I can do it!" He ran fast and made it without a slip.

Laren and I saw caribou on our way to get a Dall sheep.

This brought back a memory of a time when I was about Laren's age. This situation was not nearly as dangerous as what my dad had gotten me into, and I was glad for that.

Dad and I were climbing a cliff above the marble quarry in Marble, Colorado. This cliff was about 200 feet above the quarry hole, which was about 100 feet deep.

Looking down into the hole, all you could see was ice floating in a pool of black water in the bottom of the quarry. It was a dizzying view. There were three pitons wedged into a crack in the limestone cliff. I had to get a good solid hold and wedge my toes into a crack, then use the pitons to pull myself up and over the edge of the cliff to a ledge.

From there I could stand and climb out of the gorge. Dad had gone ahead. He turned saying, "You'll be okay, but don't look down. Just pretend there's solid ground below you and keep climbing."

I was petrified. Here I was, a 13-year-old boy, hanging on a cliff. Then I looked down. My head began to spin and I felt like throwing up. I said, "Dad, I can't do it!"

"Son, there is no turning back. Just put your head against the rock and take a moment to recover. Do not look down again, but go ahead and climb out as soon as you feel better."

After a moment I said, "Okay," and I obeyed, knowing if I didn't do exactly as I was told I would pay a huge price and fall. I made it over the rim and I was all in one piece, but I was one scared little boy.

I told Laren we would be going back to camp by a different route and we could leave that slippery chute behind.

We moved across the mountainside, which was now typical alpine tundra. We stayed high and continued traveling north on an east-facing steep, grassy slope. As we contoured around, I spotted a couple of rams. We ducked down below the horizon and they didn't see us. I told Laren about the rams, and we crawled until the slope the sheep were on came into view. Carefully peering over the horizon, I could see the sheep.

To my surprise, an even dozen rams were in a loose herd about 75 yards below us. Laren took his pack off and set up for a shot. He slipped his prostrate form over the crest of the ridge we were behind.

We tried to decide which sheep was the best trophy. It wasn't easy with so many big rams in one bunch. Finally, we picked one out and Laren steadied for a shot.

Bang! Every sheep began to run to our left over a high point and across a swale where we couldn't see them. I heard the slap of the bullet and was sure Laren had hit the ram. We got up and ran over the high ground and caught up with one of the rams. It was obviously hit.

Laren and I both shot at him as he ran directly away from us. He went down in a heap. We walked to him, and I looked down the mountainside. Standing about 200 yards below us was a mature ram. It wasn't as big as Laren's but would do nicely for me. I sat down, made the shot, and as you can guess, we now had two rams to pack out instead of one.

This may sound like we took more than we could use. But we each had a license and it was legitimate to share meat with other folks, and there were many older natives in the village who could use the meat and would be so thankful for it. We had no qualms about taking the second sheep for the leaders of the village to distribute.

Laren gets a real trophy. It measured 39 inches.

Laren and I dressed out the sheep and spent the rest of the morning caping and boning meat. We packed both rams into our packs and made the trip out to the cabin uneventfully. It was tough going, but we did as before with Lori's caribou and took many rests.

When we were almost to the cabin river crossing, our friend, Scrib flew over us with Betty in the plane. He had come to start ferrying us out to our cabin in Copper Center. He kept circling us and wriggling his wings.

We finally decided he was trying to show us something. We looked and searched the hillsides above us. Scrib flew off, and we continued to the river crossing and the cabin. Later we learned that they had spotted a large black bear about 100 yards above us. We were looking in the correct direction, but due to the topography, we just couldn't see it. This was bear country, for sure.

We were loaded with fresh meat and hiking through an area with a fairly high population of black bears and grizzlies. This is why Scrib was so intent on letting us know there was a bear so close to us. For safety, we needed to know.

The wilderness gifted us on this trip. It helped us develop survival skills that must be individually mastered, since they were undeniable rules that cannot be broken. This means a man must go with the wilderness and not fight against it. It is a harsh land and will quickly become a hostile land if basic rules of survival are violated.

I believe mankind has adapted to creation, and in his genius has developed skillful and adept survival behavior. Man has survived by living in communities and economically depending on each other.

Additionally, when two or more rugged individualists go it together and survive some of the hardships that can occur in the back country, they develop a bond of camaraderie. This solidarity and companionship between two strong males can develop into true brotherly love.

As individualists, we do not do for others what they can do for themselves, but we are quick to recognize when our combined efforts are needed. In short, the wilderness knocks the rough edges off and refines us in a way that is rarely replicated in any other setting.

It was time to go. The Super Cub lifted off the runway and the ride smoothed. Air was definitely smoother than the rock strewn landing strip. We left Mr. Weasel behind in possession of the Dadina River cabin. He had been such a stimulating cabin host. I thought, *What a great America we live in.*

The Amazing Bush Plane—Dog-Sled Team of the Sky

Chapter 5

Frozen Toes

"It's time to get up, Son!" I pulled five-year-old Laren into an upright position. "Remember, we're going on Tyler Mountain today." The sun had yet to rise, and it was one of those cold, wintry November mornings that held the high country hostage to a strict set of survival rules.

If you venture out on a cold day like this, you must dress warm, eat for heat, and do not get overheated when climbing. We started by dressing right with many layers of clothing and warm felt-lined shoe pacs for footwear. Next we ate a good hot breakfast of oatmeal, toast, and milk.

We were eager to go, but I was apprehensive about how Laren would handle the minus 10 degrees the thermometer was registering on the fence pole outside. I knew he was used to these conditions because we lived at 8,500 feet elevation, a high country environment with predictable accompanying cold temperatures. It was still a cause for concern, and I knew if we did not prepare for cold we could be in real trouble.

Laren and I hopped into the pickup after doing the chores of feeding and milking our two cows and six goats. Our destination was the base of Tyler Mountain. It was only five or six miles north of our home across the valley. From our front porch we could see the ridge we were going to climb.

Tyler Mountain as viewed from our front porch

I parked in a small meadow below a rocky ridge that had a good trail to the crest of the basin. I knew a lot of mule deer were staging for the rut.

"Laren, there are a lot of bucks on the move and they do a lot of pushing and shoving each other. Sometimes the pushing ends up in more than just a friendly game of push and shove. Sometimes it means the death of one of the contestants."

Laren was excited to see some fresh deer sign. He said, "Look, Dad, some deer poop. A deer was right here this morning!"

"It looks like more than one was here. There's more sign over here," I told Laren, and then explained, "This is the breeding season for deer, and the big bucks are looking for does to breed. Their breeding season is only a short time in the fall and is timed so that in the spring the babies are born when the weather is most favorable. If a doe isn't bred the first time then she will keep coming into heat every 21 days until she is pregnant. This makes sure that some fawns are born later in the spring in case the weather is bad during the first breeding cycle. This spreads the breeding season out. It's nature's way of preventing bad weather extremes from knocking out an entire breeding season."

We began the steep, arduous climb and stopped often to rest. I showed Laren the bitterbrush plants that provided the deer with high nutrition. We also climbed through the nutritious service berry bushes and common big sagebrush, which made up much of the high quality deer intermediate winter range in this area.

"Laren," I said, "deer are migratory here in north central Colorado. That means they move from summer range in the higher elevations to intermediate range in the fall and early winter. Then they move into the lowest elevations when deeper snows come. In the spring the reverse is true. The deer move up in elevation as the snow melts. This gives the deer the highest quality food sources throughout the year."

I enjoyed teaching our kids the biology and habits of the wildlife in our area. All the time I hoped I was instilling in them a love for the country and knowledge of wildlife as well as the ecology of the mountain environment.

The way was steep and brushy, but we were on a good game trail. We took our time climbing ever upward, stopping often to catch our breath in the frosty, high country air. Seeing some fresh deer tracks, I said, "Son, be extra quiet, especially when we take a quick look-see over this ridge."

"Okay, Dad, I'll be quiet as a mouse," he replied.

After climbing for about an hour, we sat down for a rest. All of a sudden, Laren began to cry. "I want to go home." He wanted to turn back because his feet were so cold. I took his shoes off and looked at his feet. They were nearly frostbitten and were white with cold, and I wondered how he had been tough for so long. I realized this day was too cold and harsh for Laren.

My desire to see that Laren had a good time served a good purpose. It made me more aware of Laren's needs. Right then our enemy was the intense cold, and for the first time I realized how crippling this could be. Inside my gut I actually hurt and felt shaky, and I said, "Son, we will get your feet warm right now."

I could just picture blackened toes having to be amputated, but this kind of negative thinking would get us nowhere. I quickly got hold of myself and took action. Sitting down, I pulled my shirt up and placed those frozen little toes on my warm belly. As his feet warmed, they hurt and ached so badly, but he never complained. Once his feet began warming up, he really didn't want to go home.

I said, "Son, if you need to go home we can go back right now."

"No, Dad, I'm okay now. Let's go find a deer," Laren replied.

I debated about going back, but Laren still wanted to find a deer—which is a much more agreeable task when one is all warmed up. We began the climb again, confident that if his feet became cold again, we had a solution.

"Laren," I said, "my stomach will always be the heater for you when we can't build a fire to warm you up. You could say my tummy is the heat for little feet, so don't wait so long to tell me. If your feet get cold again, we need to warm them up right away."

We were nearing the top when we decided to step over the ridge and sit to observe the area with field glasses. Carefully, I led the way to take another quick look before we sat down to glass the area. As we stepped over the edge on the big rocks, a nice four-point mulie bounded away.

He was running in a straight line from me so I was able to get a good shot. The timing was perfect and the deer dropped instantly. "Wow, that was a good shot, Dad!" Laren exclaimed.

Happy, we dressed him out and left him to cool. Later, I would return with horses to pack him out. The task of cleaning the deer in the extreme cold was enjoyable because the body heat of the buck helped warm my hands.

We returned home with a story to tell. We knew we had accomplished more than just taking a nice big buck. My son, although only five, became a young man for sure that day. Laren bragged about us getting a four-point mulie buck. I could see this was a big deal to him. My mind turned this over. We lived right in the wild country and had opportunities to see game animals on a regular basis. A lot of hunters would give their eye teeth to see a buck like this.

A four-pointer may not sound big to an eastern white-tailed deer hunter, but this deer in eastern count would be classed as a big ten-pointer and would be considered a trophy class animal. This buck was truly a beautiful animal and was nearing his old age. In fact, he would soon not be able to make it through the harsh winters we encounter nearly every year.

A fat four-pointer for our family larder

This is one benefit of hunting trophy animals. We harvest the older aged animals before they are too weak to survive. This is an aid to ensuring the health of the game animals overall.

This class of animal is best harvested as it makes room for the younger animals to carry on the breeding functions. The herd is healthier because of the harvest by man and by other predators like the mountain lion. In the overall picture, there is a balance between deer, predators, and food supply. Man is an important predator, just like wolves, mountain lions, and bears are vital to the overall health of their prey populations.

I sat on the sofa thinking. I said to Betty, "You know, old Tyler Mountain is history for us now. Yet I'll always remember how Laren and I were partners for a day of hardship and fun. We had the joy of success and conquered the extreme cold, but I have to admit it was pretty tough for a five-year-old. This hunt was one that developed his character and ethics in hunting and had all the elements of fair chase."

Laren's enthusiasm had not waned. He said, "Mom, my toes got cold, and I traded my cold toes for Dad's warm belly. I got all warmed up and then we got a buck deer." This hunt and cold feet brought a boy and his dad together in comradeship in a way that we cannot plan. These moments just happen.

The hunt turned out well and Laren did not get frostbitten or get too exhausted. We were home at an early hour, which allowed Laren to recover from the cold and made it possible for me to get a horse and pack the buck out.

I loved to hunt and wanted our children to love the outdoors and especially hunting. Therefore, I tended to involve them at a level of hardship that was above their age.

Dads need to remember to let their children have fun in outdoor endeavors. I think for the first time I could see how hard it was for me to gear myself down to a level they enjoyed.

Getting an animal was far too important to me. This story may be a good example for fathers who take their youngsters out in conditions that many grown men would have trouble coping with. I should not have expected the children to cope as well as an adult would.

It is a wonder that our kids like outdoor activities, considering the hardship of some of our ventures. But they do love to be out in the outdoors. As our family matured, I eased up on pressuring the kids. I did not force them to have the same drive to succeed that I have in order to have a successful outing. They could achieve their own level of enjoyment in God's great outdoors.

Lauren's first Alaska fish

The little man

The Little Man
By Larry Roper

Back in the recesses of my mind, a scene came to me so clear.
'Twas one of those indelible moments of a time we hold so dear.
My boy and I were climbing Tyler Mountain, cold and snowy it
      was, 'neath a cloudy sky.
Our quest was for a buck that day, just my five-year-old and I.
We stopped to get more air and my son began to cry.
I drew him close, I held him tight, and implored of him as to why.
He sobbed and stamped his little feet,
And said he wanted to retreat.
I took off his shoes and socks, and sure 'nough, his feet were so
      icy.
His toes were white with cold and were so frosty.
No longer did I need a deer,
But I had a little boy trying to hide his tear.
I pulled up my shirt and put his feet on that tummy of mine.
It wasn't long and his toes were toasty warm, now he was ready
      to climb.
We made our way up a windblown ridge to find some game
      that day.
We peaked o'er the edge to see a fat four-pointer bounding
      away.
I quickly made a very nice shot;
The buck would be meat in the pot.
My son may not remember the details that cold, cold day,
But I will always hold those little toes in my memory, safely tucked
      away.
You must know by now, the little five-year-old became a man for
      at least one day,
    And when we returned victorious, the little man was once
again a child at play.

Chapter 6
Cliffs, Goats, and No Food

"Larry! Larry! Where are you?" Now Bill was really worried. He knew we had bedded down on the exposed ridge and wrapped ourselves in flimsy space blankets. That was about two hours ago. He also believed that if a man walked in his sleep or even stumbled around in a half-awake stupor in any of three directions of the compass, he would likely fall off a cliff. He knew we were dead tired, hungry, and cold. It was a combination that could lead to restless sleep.

He called again, "Larry, where are you, man? Did you fall off the mountain?"

This time I answered. I had moved, all right, but I'll talk about that later in the story.

It had started as an adventure, for sure, at our cabin known as the "Copper Castle" at Copper Center, Alaska. We were on a spur of the moment Rocky Mountain goat hunt. The glacial, murky waters lapped at the side of the flat-bottomed riverboat.

We were about to launch into the Copper River on a sandbar below the old abandoned village of Chitina.

"Bill, are you ready for a once in a lifetime goat hunt?" I asked.

"You bet I am," he said. "I've been ready for so many years. It's like a dream."

I looked Bill right in the eye, and thinking of all the provisions we had just loaded, I said, "Bill, have you ever been forced to live without the next meal planned or provided?"

He laughed and said, "No, and I don't think I really want to!"

I said, "Well, it can be done, but I'm glad we have plenty of chuck in waterproof bags today." Why I thought of this, I will never know, but we would be put to the test on this trip.

Bill, a friend from Denver, and I were visiting Dean, a friend in Kenny Lake, Alaska. We had been talking and cooked up a spur of the moment goat hunt. Now here we were, carrying the last of our camp gear from the truck. I plopped my pack down.

Dean looked at everything we just loaded and said, "It's sure a relief to see everything shipshape and in good white-water stowaway waterproof bags. We know at least our gear will be dry even if we happen to get wet." We had already loaded 40 gallons of outboard motor gas and were ready to launch into the mighty Copper River below Chitina, Alaska.

Yes, we were ready for a goat hunt on the Copper River. In our area, goats were difficult to hunt as their habitat was remote and the terrain hard to negotiate. Getting one of the white goats with ebony black horns and hooves had been a lifelong dream for Bill. Dean knew I was always ready for any outdoor adventure. Just to be out of doors filled some kind of hidden need I had buried within me.

Dean had the riverboat and lived near Chitina; therefore, he felt no pressure to get a goat but was relishing the opportunity to be out with two Christian friends and hunt together. He wanted us to get to know each other on a deeper level.

Dean was a fur trapper and trader in the interior of Alaska and had two boys and a native-born wife from the village of Northway. With her home further north, Dean covered a large area, buying furs from scattered outposts and villages. He showed us some fine wolf furs he had just received from a tannery and, of course, Bill and I had to see his entire collection.

Betty loved the Arctic fox pelt that Dean gave her.

Dean said the quality of Alaska furs compared to what is harvested outside in the Lower 48 is strikingly superior. Alaskan fur is a result of the climatic conditions the animals live in and survive. There are plenty of cold temperatures, such as 40 to 50 below zero, through the long, dark months of winter. This produces luxurious, deep furs that are much warmer for outdoor clothing.

Of course, there are January thaws that make a person think winter is over. Then with a vengeance the cold will settle in again, and all of God's creatures are back into the weather that demands the deepest, most luxuriant fur for body heat to remain stable.

We were enjoying our education on fur trapping and the industry that is a part of our American heritage. We knew we were witnessing a way of life that was fading into oblivion. Trapping as a profession is a lost way of life due to the changes in our culture and the beliefs and attitudes of people who only see the surface regarding utilizing or harvesting fur animals.

Researchers have discovered that the balance of nature is a fluctuating balance. In general, the prey animal population responds to the predatory animal populations. For example, when the prey population increases, then the population of predators increases, also.

The inverse is not necessarily true. For example, if the deer population drops significantly, then the cougar population switches to other prey such as elk and small game. Therefore, the predator population remains high and the result is that the predators can actually have a significant effect upon the deer population, keeping it down. That's why good management includes hunting both the prey and the predator populations to manage the herd for productivity and maintain a balance. Man is a part of that balance.

In Alaska, the grizzly bear population had increased to such a level that in some localities bears killed more moose than hunters did. In some of these areas the moose population was in jeopardy, and the answer was to reduce the bear numbers. In some cases, wolf numbers need reduction since they are also efficient predators.

We got to the business at hand, which was to get on the Copper River and boat about 35 river miles down toward Cordova to get to good goat habitat. This area is roadless wilderness and lies below the confluence of the Tiekel and Copper Rivers.

Bill said, "I'll make a final check to be sure we have everything we need." He checked over his mental list. "It looks like we're ready," he said, and I agreed. We had sleeping bags, food, and my wall tent, and little did we know circumstances would bring us a situation where we would use none of the "necessary equipment."

We shoved off into the Copper River. Dean got things running smoothly and settled back to let Bill and me look for driftwood and submerged trees. Bill was familiar with the job of looking for debris. Dean was an expert at picking the right channel, and we needed his expertise as the river was spread out at least 300 or 400 yards wide.

Here's Bill, fishing on the Gulkana River, looking for trash.

Dean said, "I think I'd better describe just what we have ahead of us. Pretty soon we'll enter Wood's Canyon, where the river gets so narrow that if it weren't for the vertical rock walls on each side with no shore to stand on, I could easily throw a rock across the river. It's 30-50 feet deep and moving about eight to ten miles per hour. We'll have to go through with power to keep control and move faster than the river. This involves about two miles of canyon and treacherous water."

Dean continued, "Below the canyon, the river spreads out and slows to five or six miles per hour. We can expect to travel the 35 miles to the base campsite in about two hours."

"Well," I said, "since that's the case, we could climb up the steep mountain to the bench above the timberline where I saw goats when I scouted from the air yesterday. We just might get an evening hunt today." Both Bill and I were full of anticipation and gung ho to get going.

We arrived at a gravel bar below a steep, cascading stream that came into the Copper from the west. After looking it over, we thought we could make it up to the bench where the goats should be. We unpacked the gear and since it was midday and we still had a lot of daylight hours, we ate a quick bite. Then we gathered some equipment and started up the steep mountainside.

We decided to climb to the bench I'd seen from the air for an evening goat hunt or at least to scout the area so we could have a more productive hunt the next morning. It appeared to not be too far to timberline, so we decided to set up camp when we got back. We thought we'd make the climb in a couple of hours. We could do some trail building, also, which consisted of using Dean's machete to clear some of the weedy growth from the trail.

The ecology was different in this close proximity to the coast. The coastal climate was influencing the vegetation. Numerous glaciers were on both sides of the river. This resulted in more species of plants with higher density than farther up river. They were more adapted to a climate of heavy, deep snow cover. We contended primarily with devil's club and salal bush.

We discovered our primary enemy was the devil's club. This weed grows up to four or five feet tall and has leaves shaped like elephant ears and is covered with spines on the stems and the underside of the leaves. It is impossible to get through without clearing it out with the machete. We hacked our way up through alders, salal, and devil's club on the edge of a precarious ravine that fell off to our right.

"Wow, that water in the creek sounds so tempting. Listen. It's tumbling and gurgling like only a mountain stream can." Bill and Dean both nodded their heads in agreement. We supposed the creek was clear and cold, but there was a cliff on the edge of the little gorge the stream was in, so it wasn't possible to get water to quench our thirst.

It was hot and we were sweating freely as we chopped our way and clambered up the steep slope. In fact, it was so steep that it was hand over hand in some places. Then it would level out to about a 60-degree slope, which was hardly level.

We had been laboring for about two hours, which was our estimate of how long it would take us to get above the timberline and into the lower reaches of goat habitat. We stopped for a rest and finished off the last of the bottled water.

Dean said, "It's not worth this much effort for me to get a goat. I'd rather go back down to the river and set up a base camp and cook supper, and you can come back when you get good and ready." As far as he was concerned, Bill and I could go on and hunt.

Bill and I talked it over and figured we were about three-fourths of the way, and we both were tuned in for a goat. Bill and I normally take adequate if not ample provisions on any camping or hunting trip. We knew there was plenty to meet our needs back at the tent.

We were adventuresome and didn't mind taking a risk or two. Bill was like me when I went with an Indian friend for four days armed only with a .22 caliber rifle and no bedding or extra clothing. We had lived off muskrats and hunted almost continuously. (This story is related in Chapter 9, Sacred Hunting Grounds.)

Bill and I decided it would be more efficient to stay and finish the trail and bivouac with the minimum equipment we had with us than to return and camp in luxury.

We said, "Dean, don't worry if we don't come back until tomorrow. We might just be better off to stay up here overnight." We had no food other than some dried salmon and only two space blankets in my emergency survival kit. I felt for the first time in a long time that I had someone with me as crazy as I was. Here we were, without food or camp gear in rough wilderness, and Bill was ready to bivouac with me and make do with what we had in order to be successful in goat hunting.

Dean said he was okay with our plan, and we agreed that if we did stay overnight we'd come back down by noon the next day. I knew myself and I knew wilderness, so I said, "Dean, if for some reason we can't make it by noon, we'll fire two shots, wait 15 seconds, fire two more, wait 15 seconds, and then fire a last volley of two shots. If we need help we'll fire three sets of three shots at fifteen second intervals. Is that an okay plan?"

He agreed, so we said goodbye to Dean and turned our attention to getting through the devil's club. We took turns at the hacking. It was difficult travel, but we carved out a good trail. We knew it would be better coming back.

"Bill, this is pretty treacherous right here. Let's take our packs off and climb free hand up this rocky cliff for ten or twelve feet. Then we can haul our packs up with my rope." Bill thought that was a good idea, so he went first. The cliff didn't require technical climbing skills, but it was near enough to vertical to be dangerous with our packs on.

"The scenery is spectacular," I said. "Look across the river to the east on the other side. The ecology is similar and made just for goats." We were encouraged as we saw a few goats on the other side. We hoped that after all the work we were putting into this hunt, we would find goats where we planned to be.

We were feeling the effects of not eating or drinking enough water to give a maximum sustained physical effort. We were sure we would find water but had not seen any seeps or springs. We needed to look at the base of the cliffs where ground water seeped from underground reservoirs.

The alpine habitat is where most rivers originate as small springs. They bubble right out of the ground, usually at the base of rocks. This water has been filtered and is good for human consumption.

As the streams wend their way down to the lower country and are populated with beavers and muskrats, the probability of getting the giardia parasite increases. The filtering effect of the terrain, underlain with granite rock, gravel, and talus, would provide us with good water when we found it.

We came to a long east-west ridge, and it seemed to be the bench I had seen from the air. It was much more rugged than it had appeared from the air. The view was spectacular. To the west of us were plenty of mountains rising above us, and southwest, across a chasm, there was a huge glacier.

We walked up to the edge of the chasm and saw that there was no way for us to continue southward unless we climbed the cliffs on the west side, enabling us to go around impassable cliffs.

We studied the scene before us in the setting sun. Across the chasm we saw seven Rocky Mountain goats grazing. We watched them through the 20 power spotting scope and yearned for a way to get to them. They were about 400 yards from us, but access was denied by sheer rock canyon walls. I said to Bill, "There must be a way to get to those goats."

I heard Bill exclaim, "Hey, there's water seeping out of this little ravine at the base of the cliff."

"Finally," I said, "we can get a drink."

Glassing for goats in glacier country

The water slaked our thirst, and I ate some dried salmon to help ease my hunger. Bill said, "I'd rather go hungry. There's just something about raw fish, even if it's dried and cured, that just does not appeal to me." My Indian friends sure enjoy it and have taught me to like it. Bill had one granola bar left and relished it, nursing it along, pretending it was a full meal.

Darkness was enclosing us in a half light so typical of the northland. We decided to go to sleep in our space blankets close to each other for some heat. It was about 10:30 p.m., and the temperature was dropping probably into the low 40s. We both went to sleep, but around 1:00 a.m. I awoke shivering. I was freezing.

I wondered what would happen to a sleep walker in this area. Any direction other than west would end up in a fall off the mountain. I looked at Bill, and he appeared to be sleeping soundly. I wondered how he could sleep so well and not be frozen stiff like me.

I got up and walked over to the base of the cliff about 50 feet to the west. I noticed that the rock wall came down to a steep slope of pebble-sized gravel mixed with soil. Short willow bushes were growing about 12 inches high. It was the only source of wood on this rocky site, so a fire had not been an option.

I climbed up the slope to the base of the rock cliff. It looked like I could scoop out the dirt at the base of the cliff and get just under the rock in a hollowed out bed so I could lay prostrate when I got in position under the cliff.

Now I got a firsthand lesson in insulation, which is keeping heat in by a thick layer of material next to the body. Where I'd been sleeping I'd had little insulation, but my rock shelter reflected heat from the rock back to my body, allowing me to warm up pretty quickly. I was grateful that I'd remembered this lesson in physics.

I went right to sleep and I'm sure I would have slept until daybreak had I not been awakened a short time later by Bill calling my name. "Larry, Larry!" Bill's voice trembled, his face was tense, and his body was shaking with cold. He called out, "Where are you?"

I woke and answered him. He said he was frozen stiff, lying out exposed on the ridge where I'd been with him earlier. "Why didn't you wake me? I thought sure you'd fallen off the cliff!"

"I should have woken you, but you appeared to be sleeping soundly and comfortably and I was freezing to death. I'm sorry," I responded.

Bill climbed up and scooped out a secure place to sleep. We both slept warmer until about 3:30 a.m. The sky was beginning to gray, and we knew daybreak was just around the corner.

We gathered dry, dead branches from the miniature willows on the slope below the cliff so we could kindle a fire to help us restore our lost body heat. We heated water to drink and got ready to hunt with no breakfast for our bodies. We knew we had a rigorous day ahead of us and were filled with anticipation of finding goats within reasonable climbing terrain.

We moved out to the edge of the chasm that separated us from getting to the goats we had seen the evening before. They were out grazing and moving toward the glacier. I suggested, "Let's pray and ask the Lord to move them up above the glacier and cause them to come across the head of that impassable canyon west of the glacier."

Bill agreed and we prayed, "Lord, we could climb the cliffs to the west of us and should be able to get to the goats if you would send them across the glacier. We will climb up and meet them. Thanks, Lord." Our prayer sounded preposterous to us. But with a step of faith we began to climb the broken cliffs west of us. By faith, we had a coming rendezvous with some Rocky Mountain goats.

We climbed about an hour and found ourselves near the top on another bench. Catching our breath and resting, we looked across the basin and saw a mature goat moving at a steady pace toward us. I said to Bill, "You take him when he gets into range." Bill laid the rifle across his pack on a rock. It was a .270 Winchester of mine on which I'd installed a Timney adjustable trigger set for a light two-and-a-half pounds. Most triggers are factory set for at least three-and-a-half to four pounds of pull.

When Bill and his family came to Alaska, their objective was to help missionary families with special projects. He had not planned to hunt, and as a result didn't bring his rifle. When we decided to go hunting we loaned Bill Lori's rifle. We had known them for a number of years and they had helped put a new roof on our cabin. This hunt was a bonus for them.

As he was getting the cross hairs into position, Bill's finger pressure got heavy and he shot before he was ready. The goat bolted and went over the edge of a cliff below us. Bill and I were disappointed after all our hard climbing. We sure didn't want to go back empty handed.

We laughed it off, knowing most hunters have experienced similar events. We continued hunting across the basin and to the edge of the canyon which had been our destination. Now all we had to do was sit, watch, and wait for the Lord to direct the goats down from their lofty glacial habitat.

We got to a vantage point looking south toward the glacier next to the area where the seven goats had been grazing. We sat and searched every nook and cranny below the glacier in front of us for about 30 minutes.

"There, right over there," said Bill. "Look." I looked and sure enough, there were seven goats coming down the glacier in a direction that would bring them within 200 yards of where we sat. We believed and acted upon our belief. God had granted our unusual request, which was an exciting miracle.

We marveled at what we saw! The goats were coming down the glacier in the only place where they could cross to our side. About 200 yards from us they stopped, and we were ready for them. Bill picked out one goat and I another.

We couldn't identify if they were billy goats or nannies. We lacked experience in hunting goats and were not concerned about their gender. We just wanted to take a mature goat. Bill shot the first shot, and when I heard him shoot, I shot. In actuality, our shots were almost simultaneous. My goat dropped and I asked Bill if he'd scored. "Yeah," he replied, "mine is down." "So is mine," I said. We congratulated each other, and before we did anything else, we thanked God for such a great miracle. We then set out to see Bill's goat, as mine was farther up towards the glacier and a bit east of the line to his goat.

Bill was elated. He'd made an excellent shot with an instant kill. This is just what all hunters want. No one wants to see undue suffering, and it's part of a hunter's unwritten code of ethics to do everything in his or her power to accomplish that goal. An ethical hunter will pass up a shot that has the probability of just wounding an animal.

Bill stayed with his goat to dress it out, and I went over to my goat to take care of it. It was still early in the day, about eight in the morning. I approached my goat, which had dropped just like Bill's. I reached down to turn it over.

To my surprise, it gave a kick and reared, struggling to get to its feet. I reached out to catch it with my left hand, and I grabbed a horn, which slid out of my hand and cut my palm. Blood gushed from my hand, and now it was slick and would be hard to hold on to my rifle.

I had laid my rifle down before the goat jumped up, rolling and struggling. I was thankful I had both hands free. The goat was lunging and heading aimlessly out of control toward the cliff edge about 30 feet below where it had been lying. The drop-off was vertical and at least 200 to 300 feet down into the same canyon we had skirted on our way up to the glacier. Without thinking, I quickly jumped down below the thrashing mountain goat.

I could imagine myself being pushed over the edge. I cried out, "Oh, no! A fall will kill me for sure, but if I let go, this goat will never be mine!" So I foolishly blocked its way with my body with no thought of the nearness of the cliff.

The goat was kicking and I was holding on for dear life. Confident I could keep it where it was, I held onto the goat's horn with my non-bloody hand, and with my free hand, which was bleeding profusely, I managed to get my hunting knife out of the scabbard. How, I don't know! By this time I was on my knees sliding toward the precipice. Somehow, I was able to cut the jugular vein in the goat's throat and frantically held on for dear life.

It quit the struggle, and the tussle was over. We were about 20 feet above the cliff edge. I was full of adrenalin. My knees were skinned and oozing blood. My hand was bleeding profusely. I needed some first aid.

After a brief rest and bandaging my hand, I proceeded to skin, cape, and bone the meat. I didn't go look over the edge. I thought, *Why should I get so close to a certain death plunge? You nearly bought it that time, Roper. This may be a nice goat, but it wouldn't have been worth taking a plunge.* In my mind, I could still feel the gravel sliding under my knees. I shivered and felt nauseous.

There was much work to do, so I bent to the task at hand and started to cape the goat. Caping a pelt is a time consuming task, but in the end it saves the packing of extra bone and flesh that are unusable.

To cape an animal, you skin it from the shoulders forward and completely take off the skin from the head. This can be tanned and then used by a taxidermist to make a trophy mount. All fat must be removed, and the fleshy parts of the lips need to be split on the inside so they will dry and tan effectively.

We had killed large mature nannies. Each goat had horns about nine inches long and were good trophies. After packing the boned meat and the capes, we thought we each had a load of about 85 to 90 pounds, which was a mighty heavy load. It was near maximum for us to get down off the mountain without a mishap.

Going back down the mountain was slow progress and required many stops to rest. It was particularly difficult in the places where we had to take off the packs and lower them on ropes to bypass small cliffs that were nearly vertical. We finally got back to the shrub tree line and descended down to the trail we had so laboriously hacked the day before.

About halfway down both of us were out of energy, famished for food, and as dry as if we were on the Mojave Desert without water. I was sitting on a steep hill in brush over my head. I thought, *Oh, Lord, I feel I've about had it. I need strength and I need water. Please show me the way. Renew my strength as the eagles. Help me walk and not faint.*

I opened my eyes and looked up. Unbelievably, I saw I was sitting under a high bush cranberry loaded with fruit. I exclaimed, "Bill, look what we have!" We could hear the stream below, but it was impossible to get to it. It was just tantalizing us with the sound of music made only by a clear, cold, rushing stream.

We ate as much of the berries as we could and felt somewhat renewed. Both of us believed we could go on, and we continued down the mountain holding onto limbs of alders to help us not fall or slip.

We were getting near the point where we could not go on without a major rest stop. Just when it seemed we were drawing our last breath, we plopped to the ground. We heard a noise below, but we were so tired and worn out, neither of us felt like getting up to see what was coming. We just sat there waiting for whatever.

To our surprise Dean showed up, climbing up the steep slope through the devil's club and salal brush. It was like a dream where he just materialized out of thin air. He was a sight for sore eyes, like a big brother showing up just in time to save his little brothers from the depths of exhaustion.

Dean's grin revealed his enthusiasm for helping us out. Cheerfully he said, "I was watching from the camp with my binoculars and saw you coming across the bare ridge just above the timberline. I knew you needed some help when I saw your staggering pace. It was obvious you were heavily loaded."

Bill replied, "You have no idea how grateful I am to see you and hear your voice, so warm and full of vigor!"

"I second that!" I added. Dean had water and granola bars, and we took a well-deserved break. From there on, we rotated packs so Bill and I could take turns going part of the way without a load.

At last we made it to the camp. Dean had the tent set up and had a campfire with some embers still smoldering. We added some wood and blew it back into life for a quick meal. We ate and discussed our plan.

Dean said he'd had a good time and felt rested and restored from the busy schedule he'd been keeping. He said he didn't feel the need to get a goat, and the trip was already a success to him. How could one beat the scenery and solitude provided in this place?

Bill said, "I'm glad we're able to get home early, because I was going to have to reschedule our Denver flight and take a later flight. I also need to get back to my family." Bill's wife and five children were waiting in Copper Center, staying with Betty in our cabin. "I'm sure they're tired and ready to stop living out of suitcases, let alone having to drive to Anchorage in a hurry to catch a plane," he said.

We knew they were crowded and tired after four weeks. Bill and Johnye had helped us put a new roof on our cabin, had done some fishing, and had enjoyed Alaska. Our hunt for Rocky Mountain goats was a bonus to an already great trip. Our goat hunt, in fact, was a once in a lifetime adventure!

We packed up camp, loaded the boat, and nosed it out into the mighty Copper River. We were running well, and calculated we'd make the 35 miles back to the landing by 10:00-10:30 p.m.

After another hour of running upstream against the current, loaded a bit heavier with two goats on board, Dean announced, "We're not going to make it." He'd been keeping track of the rate we had been using gas and considered the fact that we still had to go through Woods Canyon.

"What should our plan be?" We asked. "What are our options?"

We decided it would be best to get as far as we could and hope that would be at least to the bottom of Woods Canyon. I thought, *Oh, no, not another problem!* Dean said, "We could beach it below the abandoned railroad tracks that come through the tunnel adjacent to the canyon. Then after a rest, we could walk on the railroad bed the six or seven miles to the pickup."

"I don't know if I can walk that far without a good rest," Bill replied.

Joining in the conversation, I said, "I don't relish the thought of that long of a hike after what we've already been through."

However, we all knew the wilderness, and the Copper River would not give in to softness. Either we would go with what was given or we would perish.

Dean said, "I don't like succumbing to just what feels good."

Bill replied, "I'm sure not giving up either, and I'll be right there taking my share of the load."

Bill and I decided to pray about our gas consumption. Dean said he believed in prayer, but facts are facts and mechanical things are mechanical things. You just do not see God going around giving Christians good gas mileage. He said he wished he could share our faith.

Bill said, "Yeah, it's not the norm, but God is God and He will do what He pleases. We know His answer will be for our good in the long run."

We prayed and asked the Lord to extend our mileage. We didn't care how it got done, but we expected to make it safely through Woods Canyon. We began to pay close attention to our gas usage.

We measured the use by the number of minutes a five-gallon tank would last. To our relief, the next five-gallon can went twice as long as it had been going. We could only explain it in God terms. He did it, and we don't know how. In fact, to us it was not important as to how; what was important was that God was showing His great love toward us, even if we might have had some wee bit of doubt.

The canyon was coming, and we put our last two-and-a-half gallons in the fuel tank. Dean said, "It'll be touch and go, but we just might make it through to the landing. It's only a couple of miles above the mouth of the canyon." We breathed another prayer.

We buzzed on through the canyon and missed a few submerged trees in the process. I'd say we were confident yet scared as we kept going. By this time it was nearly 10:30 p.m. The stars were beginning to shine brightly, and we could see the northern lights playing in the sky above our parked truck. Dean ran right onto the sandbar, and we didn't even get our feet wet getting out of the boat. We hurriedly loaded our gear into the pickup.

Dean suggested he leave the boat and come back the next day, as Bill and I had about 65 miles to go and he had only 17 miles to his house. We agreed, especially knowing that Bill and his family needed to take off for Anchorage. They needed to leave at least by 7:00 a.m. in order to not miss their flight out of Anchorage.

I often wondered why God worked so miraculously in this particular goat hunt. We saw Him literally drive the goats across a glacier! We saw Him open our eyes to fruit when we needed it. We saw Him provide Dean with the insight to look at just the right time to see us heavily laden and then climb to meet us. We saw God take a gas engine and make it work more efficiently!

In fact, when Dean picked up the boat, he measured how much gas was left in the tank. It had a half cup of liquid, and half of that was sludge and water. There were too many things prayed for specifically to be just coincidence. God answered prayer for us. I am reminded of Psalms 37 where, in the first few verses, God tells King David that if he commits his way to God and trusts in Him with all his heart, God will bring forth His righteousness as the light and His judgment as the noon day sun, as well as give him the desires of his heart.

Pack Animals Extraordinaire!

Chapter 7

The Toughest Pack Animal, Bar None

"I have a problem," I told Betty. "Here we are in Alaska with all kinds of opportunity for getting our yearly meat supply. However, there are just no efficient ways to transport game from the field to the freezer. Most Alaskans have some kind of ATV, but those iron horses are expensive and not as dependable as our own two feet or a good pack horse. Horses I understand, and as far as I'm concerned, they're the best way to take big game."

"You've been spoiled by owning some great pack horses and riding stock," Betty replied.

"Yeah, I know, but now it's up to me to do the packing," I pointed out. You see, the things I missed the most in hunting and traveling the back country of Alaska were pack horses and saddle stock for riding and transporting camp gear.

Betty said, "What can we do? We can't afford a horse."

"Well, Pastor McKinley says they used to pack their dogs in the summer. We love dogs, and we have a dog team. I think I'll investigate how to pack dogs," I commented. Pastor Jim McKinley was the Native pastor we worked with in Copper Center.

"That sure sounds like a good idea," Betty replied.

The northern tundra and taiga forests are full of muskeg, swamps, and fens. Horses often are not practical, and winter feed for them is out of sight. I was left with one choice, and that was walking and packing mile after mile in and out of the taiga forests and tundra habitats. So I was alert for a solution. I discovered that many of the old-timers in the Native villages remembered times past when they used sled dogs during the summer and fall to pack their belongings.

In the summer these Indians camped along the Copper River, fishing with their fish wheels. A fish wheel has a net on its paddles and looks like a Ferris wheel. The paddles turn the wheel, powered by the current of the river it's in. The net scoops salmon swimming upstream. With the current turning the wheel, the fish slide out of the net into a holding box. Several hundred fish can be caught in one night using a wheel.

Building fish drying racks in fish camp

Betty and I decided that pack dogs were worth a try. What we discovered was worth more than precious rubies. It was a gem of a solution. Good pack dogs are amazing animals. They are loyal, eager, and strong. Plus, they provide safety in bear country and are loving companions. We never felt lonely or isolated as long as we had our dogs with us.

Dogs have been faithful companions, and people have put them to work, for eons. They have aided in survival and economic gains throughout human history. People became so efficient in using dogs that many specialized breeds have been developed. To name a few, there are Bernese mountain dogs, Rottweilers, Saint Bernards, and Newfoundland breeds that were bred to be draft animals.

In addition, many herd dog breeds are specialized working dogs and can be used to pack cargo. There are other examples, but with so many sled dogs in Alaska, why not double their usefulness and use them to pack, as well? The larger Malamute sled dogs used primarily for freighting and pulling contests are ideal.

When fall approached, the Athabascan Indians in the Copper River region lived what was known as a "seasonal round." They moved throughout the year to live near the resource to be harvested for each season. In the fall they moved to the caribou and moose hunting grounds. When they got their meat, they cured it by sun drying. Then as the seasons changed, the people moved to cabins built on their trap lines. They moved again in the spring to hunt muskrat and beaver. They completed the round when they arrived back at their fishing camps after the spring muskrat hunting. Dogs were a vital part of their lifestyle.

Betty packs along with the dogs.

These seasonal rounds are no longer part of the Native Alaskan way and are becoming a lost part of their culture. Most villages are now located near or on the old fish campsites. The old-timers remember the migratory habit and how dogs were packed in spring, summer, and fall and then used for hauling goods and supplies on sleds in winter. They were pleased to see me carrying on the tradition of the seasonal round using pack dogs to bring meat into the winter encampment.

We got acquainted with a non-Native family in the village who used malamute dogs for packing when they went on camping trips. We got some ideas from them and discovered we could buy good commercial dog packs.

Future pack dogs/sled dogs

King, a future pack dog for the Ropers

Our first pack trip with the dogs was a short one. Laren and his high school friend Randy and I packed into a muskeg lake about two miles from the road. We planned to hunt muskrats most of the night. We took enough food and gear for a two-night stay.

We put about 35 pounds on each dog, and they did wonderful. In fact, the dogs acted as though they had packed all their lives, bringing great joy to themselves as well as to us. We had one malamute and a black Labrador retriever. They packed equally well.

Skipper, our Lab, stood quietly as we put his pack on. His tongue was lolling out as he panted, and I was concentrating on the tie knot when he quickly whapped me on the face with his big wet tongue. "Thanks a lot, big boy!" I exclaimed as I wiped my face off. The boys laughed and thought it was pretty funny.

As soon as Skipper was loaded, he lay down while I began to pack King. He stood taller than Skipper and was one tough dog. As soon as King was packed, we donned our own baggage and hiked off through the taiga forest. It was May and the ice had just gone out on the small fen lakes.

I was hiking ahead of the boys and King was about eight or ten feet ahead of me. I heard him growl and the hackles on the back of his neck raised up in alarm. I looked up and standing facing us were two grey wolves about 150 feet away. They were beautiful and I stopped, saying, "Boys, look at the wolves," but by the time they looked up the wolves had wheeled around and disappeared into the forest. What amazed me was how they were marked similar to King.

We learned how to pack the dogs.

We weren't in danger, but the incident served to help me realize how much safer we were in the bush with the dogs along.

My next discovery was to learn that I could fly the dogs into remote areas so they could pack for me. I found in most cases that 40 to 45 pounds was the maximum weight for 75- to 80-pound dogs to carry. At first, I thought this would be an overload, but through trial and error I discovered it was okay.

Now we had access into remote areas.

The dogs could go all day staying right with me in rough sheep and caribou country. What amazed me most was how eager they were to do the work. All we had to do was take a pack in our hand and the dogs would start barking, wriggling all over, and wagging their tails with joy. They knew we were going "adventuring" again.

An example of how valuable pack dogs are and how much labor they save was a moose hunt on the upper Chistochina River. Scrib was flying us in. I had talked him into taking the dogs in the Super Cub. He was a bit doubtful at first, but the three dogs lay in the area behind the pilot seat and gave him no trouble at all.

My daughter Lori and I flew in separately to the upper Middle Fork. Lori was one of those special kids who had a lot of self-confidence. She knew who she was and what she wanted, and she wasn't easily intimidated by hardship or danger. She was in her sophomore year in high school, was on the varsity basketball team, and was active socially. This moose hunt was a highlight for her, and she was gung ho and ready for an adventure.

We put about 120 pounds of gear on the dogs and backpacked ten miles downriver where we had spotted a big bull on our flight into the airstrip. With each dog packed, Lori and I had a more enjoyable hike. The dogs carried our camp gear while we packed our groceries. We planned to hunt the next day along the west side of the river.

The morning after our trip in was a bluebird day. The birds were singing just before daybreak. The air was crisp. Sounds carried clearly and could be heard distinctly from a distance. About a half mile up the river, a cow moose was calling her long, drawn out mating call. "Lori, hear that? It's about a half mile away. Let's hone in on the sound, and we should be able to sneak to within 50 to 100 yards of the moose."

We left the dogs in camp and started out toward the sound of the mating moose. Lori said, "Dad, this is just like sneaking on that caribou. Boy, this is fun."

We crept closer and closer, and we knew we should be near the moose. "Lori, where there's a cow in heat, there just has to be a bull close by. Keep your eyes peeled."

I could see that Lori was intent and using her best sneak tactics. "There, Dad, there they are," she whispered. I could hear the excitement in her voice. Three cows saw us at the same time we saw them, and they began to run off through the brush.

The cows saw us first.

Behind them, unaware of anything other than a cow in estrus (her heat period, when she wants to be bred), a large bull whirled around to follow the cows. The bull was trotting broadside through buffalo berry bushes in the scattered spruce taiga forest. We quickly took aim, shooting almost simultaneously.

Lori's first words were, "Oh, no! I shot at the moose! But where's Dad? Did I shoot Dad? All I could see was the moose!" She breathed a sigh of relief when she heard me say, "You got him!"

The bull was down. Lori said, "I know I missed him."

"No, Lori, I don't think you missed. He was too close to you, and if you saw hair in the scope, you got him." Later I discovered her bullet embedded in the moose, proving she did get that bull.

At any rate, we had a lot of meat on the ground. It was a mature bull with a 61-inch antler spread. A bull this size would be about 500 to 600 pounds of boned meat, and that translates into a lot of packing.

I know hunters who would give their eye teeth for a chance at a bull moose this size. Lori, at age 14, had a trophy of a lifetime. Lori exclaimed, "I'm so excited! The kids at school will never believe I got this big old bull!"

Lori's bull

"The fun is over," I said. "Now we settle down and get to work. We get the fun of skinning, boning the meat, and packing it out. It's a lot of work, but then, most things in life that are worthwhile cost a lot either in labor or in dollars and cents."

Lori and I worked together skinning and preparing the moose for packing. We loaded the dogs and ourselves and took the first trip out to our camp. The next four days were spent in hard labor, packing meat 10 miles to the gravel bar airstrip. I had three dogs, which I loaded for each trip, and I made one round trip a day.

Lori and I hiked back to camp and got the dogs. We loaded the dogs with about 40 pounds each and good loads on our pack frames. We took a couple of loads down to the river bottom, and we stayed the second night in the spike camp. A spike camp is a second camp away from the main camp and usually less refined. In our case, the main camp was at the airstrip and was set up by Scrib.

The next day we packed a full load to the base camp at the airstrip. Lori was proud of herself, as she packed about 30 pounds of meat. She stayed at the airstrip while I went back for a second load. I got back to camp late, after dark. I was exhausted and was pleasantly surprised that Lori had fixed a hearty supper.

She said, "I got pretty nervous and concerned that you were as late as you were, and I was a bit scared to be in camp all alone for the afternoon. I saw fresh bear sign close by, and that worried me. But I knew I had my rifle, and I was sure I'd be okay."

I said, "Lori, you will sure be able to do anything you want in your life with that kind of courage."

This short conversation is what I call a window of opportunity. A father doesn't get that kind of interaction with a teenage daughter often. This is one of the extra benefits the wilderness has to offer. When out in nature together, a father and daughter are able to connect in ways that are tough to replicate in civilization.

The next morning Lori stayed in camp waiting for Scrib to fly in and take her back to Copper Center so she could return to school. She was a brave 14-year-old, staying alone in a tent in the wilderness waiting for a plane in bear country. Lori had already proved herself on other hunts. She was a good shot.

We all carried our fair share

Base camp

Scrib came and flew her out. I had left camp early and was packing a full load back to the base camp when they flew over. I waved good-bye to them and started on my way loaded with meat.

Then I noticed something was wrong. Looking around, I realized one dog was missing. After whistling and calling several times, she finally yelped. I laid my pack down, tied the other dogs, and hiked back to investigate.

About 200 yards back up the trail I found Tikani. She was on her back with a pack tie-down rope caught on a root. I approached her and said, "Tikani, what are you doing, lying here so quiet and still, not even struggling?" She wagged her tail and looked up at me with her big, doleful brown eyes. Her look seemed to say, "Boss, I knew you'd come back soon, so I just waited for you." She had complete trust in me. This makes me take dog ownership seriously.

I put her back on her feet and we took off. She was a grateful dog, seemingly none the worse for the incident. This situation reinforced in me the value of having the dogs with me in the back country. We really were a team, looking out for each other. The dog was more than just a canine work animal. She was my friend and my companion. She trusted me and I trusted her.

We finished the trip without incident. On the fourth day when I approached the kill, I detected something was changed. The carcass had been moved. Sure enough, a grizzly had found the kill and had covered it with leaves, moss, and sticks in a mound about eight feet in diameter. I examined the carcass and found I now had only a small amount of meat to pack.

After three days of hard labor packing meat, I was more than willing to share some meat with a bear. The grizzly had taken all but about ten pounds of good meat, so I threw it in my pack and let the dogs scamper ahead light as a feather. What a relief to know I did not have to make the distance fully loaded.

The pack dogs gave me safety, and it was a great benefit. A good pack dog for the wilderness traveler is truly man's best friend and can mean the difference between survival and perishing in the wilderness.

The safety factor is one of the most important things about having good dogs in camp. Unless they're cornered or have cubs to protect, bears usually run from dogs. Dogs have tremendous noses and can detect a bear before we are aware it's in the immediate vicinity. I found that the more I used dogs, the more I watched them and let them tell me what lay ahead.

The dogs will let you know there's game in the area. I believe if guides and outfitters used dogs to pack and be companions, they would have another drawing card for clients.

The safety and aesthetic values of having good working dogs in camp outweigh any disadvantage. My dogs loved me, and I loved them. They were not just mine; every member in the family loved the dogs. Somehow, they complete our lives and teach us how to love and be faithful.

Companions taking a break   Betty loves little pack dogs

Pack dogs carry meat, hunters carry antlers—King, a great pack dog

Chapter 8
Kachemak Bay Scores Big

We drove into Dale's place at Homer, Alaska, in the early morning. The dew was heavy on the grass, and the sun was up in the northland. My dad said, "I have never seen anything like this house, and come to think of it, I'll probably never see one like this again." Dad was a building contractor and looked at all buildings through the eyes of a finish carpenter. This building's construction satisfied the occupants, for sure, but it was atrocious as far as meeting building standards.

Even though the day looked like it could be sunny and warm, it was a sun that was weak and not even warm enough to burn off the dew. Betty, Laren, Lori, and I had traveled from Glennallen to the Kenai Peninsula and camped in camper trailers with my mom and dad, who were visiting us from Colorado. We had been told that Dale was the man to contact about where to fish in Kachemak Bay. Having never met him, we didn't know what to expect.

As we approached his house, we could see that Dale was obviously a "do-it-yourselfer," independent soul. The entrance to the house was through a sunken greenhouse, and there were lots of plants of various edible garden varieties. I knew at once we could survive in this place. Upon entering the house we discovered a sunken kitchen floor with an old kitchen range, a wood box, and a decidedly lived-in appearance. The house was certainly unique.

After introductions and small talk, we got down to the reason that we came to Dale's home. I said to Dale, "We've heard so much about how terrific the fishing is near Homer in Kachemak Bay that we want to try it out firsthand. Two of our teenagers are with us and are looking forward to a boating adventure." We had a five-man Achilles rubber raft with a ten-horsepower engine.

As we talked, Dale suggested he take his foldboat and his small 14-foot aluminum fishing boat and go with us. His two teenage girls could pilot the small fishing dory while Dale would go in his foldboat with one of our kids riding with him. That way, we could all go without overloading any one boat.

We used an Achilles raft and a foldboat.

Kachemak Bay, here we come!

At the Kachemak Bay Lodge, we loaded our equipment into the boats and pushed off after saying we would be back around 6 or 7 p.m. I looked at the faces of the kids, and I could see the excitement building as we motored out towards Bird Rock. "Look, Dad!" Laren exclaimed. "I see an Orca, a killer whale. Hey! There's more!" Then Lori enthusiastically added, "Over there, what are they? Oh! It's sea lions!"

Getting ready to go out and fish at Homer, Alaska

Rain gear is a must.

It was still early, about midmorning, and we had all day to play, fish, or do whatever struck our fancy. We were passing Bird Rock, aptly named, as it was covered with sea birds. Most of the birds were auks nesting on the moss-covered, rough, nearly vertical cliffs. At the base of the cliffs on the rocks where the surf hit, sea lions lounged about. Seals followed us as we cruised along. Sea otters were also known to frequent the area, but we didn't see any.

After a couple hours of travel in the boats, the far shore came into view. Dale said, "Right here is probably a good place to fish."

Right away, Laren shouted, "I got one, I got a fish!" After he reeled it in, we could see that it was a small salmon. We caught several more salmon and a small halibut, along with a few rock fish and sculpins.

We beached the boats at a likely looking beach that had some driftwood for a fire and a few larger rocks for a fire pit. We built a fire and used a flat rock for a reflector oven to cook salmon and halibut that we filleted. It wasn't long before I called out, "Come and get it before I throw it away!" It hadn't taken long to cook a fine lunch. With some bread and butter to go along with the fish, a better meal would be hard to find anywhere.

A better meal you could not find.

After eating, we had a great time combing the beach, watching seals, fishing, and just taking it easy. We were oblivious to the sky, which was warning us of danger. If we'd have looked, we would have seen the big black thunderheads in the northwest. However, the first indication we noticed that trouble was brewing was the wind beginning to blow and the sea swells getting larger.

The wind had a clear message for us: Get ready for a storm and, if possible, get back to the shore where you came from. Dad exclaimed, "Look at that sky. It's getting black, and this wind is bringing it to us pretty doggone fast."

Dale exclaimed, "Uh-oh, we're in trouble! Those clouds and wind are telling us to get off the bay as soon as possible. It's not fun to be caught on the water in a storm like this."

"Well, you're the guy who ought to know," I said. "Let's get going!" The wind was really developing into a gale, and we could feel the moisture in the air.

The smart thing would have been for us to wait out the storm and put our efforts into building a good shelter on the shore, but we erroneously thought we needed to beat the storm and get back to the lodge.

Feverishly, we loaded the boats as the wind was beginning to blow with gale force. A fine rain settled in with serious intent to do us in.

We were about halfway across the bay past Bird Rock when the foldboat's engine failed. Dale could not get it started. He yelled, "Come and get me! I have no power!" I steered my raft over next to his foldboat. My dad got a good hold of the boat, and Lori, who was riding with Dale, also got a good hold of our raft.

My ten-horsepower Johnson outboard was running like a champ. By this time, the waves were at least ten feet high, and we were fighting a rip tide. In order for me to make any headway, I would point the raft toward the trough between the waves. Then, as a wave would start to go over the top of us, I would steer the boat perpendicular to it, riding over, and then drop into the next trough and repeat the process again and again.

I yelled at Dad, "Hang on, we're in for it! I've never seen anything like this!"

Dad looked at me, and I could see his genuine worry and apprehension. He said, "What are we going to do?"

I yelled. "We can pray, and I'll keep on fighting to make it to shore."

Dad held on to the foldboat and Lori held on to our Achilles raft. Meanwhile, Dale pulled and pulled on the starter but could not get the foldboat's little outboard motor to fire up and run.

Several hours passed as I held our zigzag course, moving slowly toward the beach. We were just holding our own.

Darkness had come sometime after midnight. Remember, in this part of Alaska in the summer, night time looks more like twilight. You have to go farther south to find complete darkness. I could see that Lori's face was tight and drawn with fear and worry. She asked, "Do you think we'll make it to shore?"

"Where are your girls, Dale?" I had lost sight of them back at Bird Rock in their small boat. "Are they familiar with how to keep afloat in waves like this?" Dale was not too sure, even though he thought they were pretty competent. We prayed, "Lord, keep them safe and deliver them to the beach."

We were too cold and busy to pay any attention to our fear, but it was a harrowing experience for all of us. Fear was there in our minds and worry for the girls' safety was hanging over us all. It was most prevalent in Dale as he spoke with a voice that was all choked up. He said, "I hope they're okay, but there's nothing I can do without my outboard motor running. I fear the worst for them."

After so many hours, I could see Lori, Laren, Dad, and Dale beginning to get mild hypothermic symptoms. They were starting to shiver, and we were all getting soaked to the skin, even though we had rain gear.

Hypothermia is a condition in which the body cannot maintain its normal temperature. We were all losing body heat in the wet, driving rain and the continuous dousing we took from the huge waves.

Hypothermia has several stages. First, a person gets cold all over and begins to shiver. Following this stage is a feeling of extreme lethargy. Usually the skin gets pale and a clammy sweat occurs. Then the fingers get numb, white, and stiff. Dexterity and body movements become slow and awkward and the person can't move easily or quickly.

If a person goes into the next stage, then the possibility of death is imminent. It is a time of feeling sleepy, and then a feeling of warming up comes over the person, which lulls the person into going to sleep. Death follows soon if the person is not treated for hypothermia. The main treatment is to get hot liquids into the person and then immerse the entire body in a hot bath. Our crew was in the early stages; their lips were blue and their muscles were shivering, but they still had fair control of their coordination and thinking.

Finally the shore came into view, but we had no idea where we were. Nevertheless, finding any beach to land on was the most important thing in our lives at that time. We landed and dragged the raft and foldboat up higher on the shore. Terra firma felt pretty good to our feet!

About 300 yards from the beach, we saw a car drive by, and we realized our beach was parallel to the road and not far from the lodge where the women were waiting.

Dad and Dale took the kids to the road while I launched back into the bay to traverse down the shoreline toward the lodge to look for Dale's girls or signs of their boat. We were probably three or four miles from the lodge and the dock. About 30 minutes later I spotted their boat pulled up on the beach. I could not see the girls, but I could see that they had landed and so I assumed they were safe.

I kept going down the bay about 100 yards out from shore, looking for the lodge. About 200 yards from the dock I prayed, "Lord, help me get through these breakers." Boats that were moored at the dock were being tossed about as though they were matchsticks. Some were damaged from hitting other boats.

I was making progress toward the dock when I heard a crack like a baseball bat hitting a hard ball solidly. It was my prop! I had hit a submerged rock and the pin sheared. "Lord, what am I going to do? I'm at the mercy of the sea!" I could feel the pull of the riptide. I was headed out to sea.

My mind was racing. *Now they will all be looking for me. They think this ordeal is over, but I have screwed it up good.* Frantically, I began to paddle, but I made no headway at all. *I have to get back to the lodge*, I thought. Even though I was about all in, I knew I had to keep up the fight a bit longer.

It is amazing to me how a person somehow comes up with reserve strength when they are at the end of their rope. I was at that point. All I could do was tie a knot in my rope and hang on with all my might. It was then that I prayed, "Lord, stop the storm and help me get back to the dock."

I cried out again to the Lord, "Stop this wind! Calm this sea and save me!" Miraculously, the wind died down and the waves abated. "Oh, thank you, thank you!" God had answered my prayer of desperation. I began to put all my remaining energy into paddling back to the dock. I was fearful the wind might start up again, and I couldn't risk going at it again.

Soon I was at the dock and I tied up the raft. I got my stiff, cold body out of the raft, and for a minute I just stood there. It was hard to believe that I was safe. But I still didn't know if Dale's girls were okay for sure. I made my way to the lodge.

There in the large lobby warming themselves by the fireplace stood our whole crew. The two girls were there and seemingly were okay.

It was a wonderful feeling to experience the end of the nightmare and feel the relief that goes through your body. I felt a bit numb to reality and was so happy, but I was near tears. In short, I felt as though someone had taken a big fire hose, turned it on full blast, and washed me inside and out. I think I needed to go to sleep and not wake up until the whole thing was over. The trip along the shore looking for sign of the two girls was a trip I never want to make again.

We learned that Betty had called the State Troopers, and they were organizing a search party. They had been waiting for the weather to abate, as it would have been impossible to see or fly the way the weather had been. Everyone was only too glad to call off the rescue efforts.

After eating a good hamburger, we bade Dale and his girls farewell, then we got into our campers for a well-deserved sleep.

The next day we traveled back to Copper Center, much wiser and very grateful. We had deeper faith in the Lord's care for each of us as individuals. In fact, we felt a bit like Peter must have felt when he walked on water. Like Peter, we needed to keep our eyes on Jesus. There is nothing like the power of water in a storm to convince us of the power of God!

Chapter 9

Sacred Hunting Ground

In order to protect the families represented, this chapter purposely does not delineate exact geographical boundaries or provide actual names. The Athabascan Indians are protective of the ancient properties claimed by their clans. For this reason, the names of people, places, and geographic sites are fictional. We want to do everything we can to maintain the trust given us by the family represented. It was indeed an honor to be shown this area as well as to be able to hunt in a traditional manner for muskrats during the spring breeding season.

◀▶◆◀▶◆◀▶◆◀▶◆◀▶

Joe entered his friend's cabin. "We borrow your canoe," he said. "We bring it back in few days."

Wow! I thought. *That was some negotiation!* The request didn't include "please" or "thank you," there was no explanation of why we needed the canoe, and Joe didn't say specifically when we would have it back. The deal was made based upon trust and a man's word. It was the ultimate contract.

This negotiation was a cultural phenomenon showing how status and trust work in Indian clans and how it carries over into relationships with the white man.

Joe knew which friend to ask for the use of a 20-foot freight canoe. It was a Grumman aluminum canoe able to pack three men and a dog and their take of muskrats.

We borrowed the canoe, with a ten-horsepower Mercury engine mounted on its square transom, for the trip into Joe's ancestral hunting ground. Our goal was to shoot as many muskrats as possible and market the furs. Joe invited another Indian friend, Elvin, from another clan. They both attended the chapel where Betty and I served as missionaries.

Thinking back, I remembered my communication with Joe about making this trip with him.

"What shall I bring?" I asked.

111

"Just you and a .22 rifle," he answered.

"Is that all? Shall I bring a bedroll or some food?" I asked.

He looked at me, grinned, and said, "No. Leave at home. We need room for furs and meat. We go Indian way."

"Okay," I said. "Is it all right to bring our big black Labrador retriever? He can really help us retrieve muskrats from the small streams and lakes."

"Yes, bring your dog if he doesn't bite."

I said, "He won't bite unless your leg smells like a muskrat."

Joe raised an eyebrow, and when he discerned I was teasing, he grinned and said, "Dog may bite and may not return."

I think I was being tested to see if I could make the grade. Not many guys would want to venture into the wilderness on a canoe trip during high water with nothing more than a .22 caliber rifle and the clothes on their back.

We took the canoe to the river landing just below Joe's cabin, then stepped in after loading 20 gallons of outboard motor fuel, the dog, and some warm coats. I was appointed chief navigator and ran the engine and guided the boat through the troubled waters. Joe was self-appointed "Chief" of the expedition, and Elvin sat in the bow looking for floating and semi-submerged logs in the spring runoff river.

The river was running bank to bank, swollen and fuming with spring flood water. The water was murky and was carrying a lot of trash from tree sweeps that had come loose from the banks. The sweeps, logs, and limbs had fallen into the swollen, angry waters rushing out to sea. I depended on Elvin and his quick decisions as he pointed out hazards in the boiling, angry waters.

We traveled most of the day up the river and about mid-afternoon we made a stop. Joe took us to a place overgrown with brush. It was here that he grew up. It was a road-less area. He showed us the remnants of the cabins and took us down to the river edge and said, "This is where we dry fish." Old fish drying rack poles were strewn about.

Then he pointed. "Over there across the river in the muskeg swamps is where we trap muskrat, mink, beaver, and otter. We go there next, and we shoot muskrat and eat supper."

Of course, the menu was obvious. It was muskrat, skewered on a stick and roasted over hot coals. Muskrat is good food. It tastes a lot like rabbit, but is a darker meat.

Native to North America and Europe, muskrats are large amphibious rodents about the size of a cottontail rabbit. They are closely related to the vole and the lemming, with a thick brown coat and musk glands. Muskrats are the largest rodent in the rat family, and they can be up to 24 inches long from the tip of the tail to the tip of the nose. They can weigh up to three-and-a-half pounds.

They are prolific, having up to 11 young per month, and in Alaska they breed from late spring through the summer months.

Muskrats eat tubers, pond weeds, cattails, water lilies, fish, and mussels, and during stress periods they may be cannibalistic. They make burrows and dome shaped houses of weeds and rushes. In winter they forage under the ice and build pushups in the ice in order to get air to breathe and have a place to rest. A pushup is kept open and does not freeze shut through constant use of the muskrat, which is active both day and night. They have pushups throughout their territory in the frozen-over lake or pond.

They are similar to beaver in that they can stay under water several minutes. The muskrat's dense fur has a soft, luxurious undercoat that stays dry when it is in the water.

According to the National Geographic Society in *Wild Animals of North America* (1960), they were America's number one fur bearer. At that time they supplied more than six million pelts annually in North America.

The Native Americans living in the north use them for various articles of clothing. Hats and mittens top the list. In some southern states the meat is considered a delicacy and a gourmet food.

We crossed the river and beached the canoe on a sand bar, then hiked inland to the swampy muskeg, which was typical pothole terrain. The ponds were interlaced and more of the surface was water than land.

Dry land was particularly scarce to find, and we were walking on muskeg mosses and lichens on swampy ground.

Whenever we took a step the surface would shake and your foot would sink in four or five inches. Where there was dry ground, it was underlain with permafrost, and the spruce trees were stunted, typical of the taiga forest. Needless to say, there was an abundance of mosquitoes.

We walked inland from the river about a mile, finding ourselves in perfect muskrat habitat. The ice had melted in the ponds, and muskrats were on the move in their home ranges. At this time of year they were in the height of their breeding season. The rats (a common nickname) were fighting each other and mating. They often had deep cuts in their pelts where their long, curved, yellowed incisor teeth had slashed through the skin in a fight with another rat.

Joe told Elvin and me to go ahead and hunt. He would start a fire so we could come back later and eat skewered muskrat meat. He busied himself skinning some of the muskrats we had already killed.

Hunting muskrats

Elvin and I took different routes to hunt the ponds. I shot two or three muskrats with Skipper retrieving them for me. I took a step while searching a pond for the "V" wake a swimming rat would make as it crossed the pond to investigate my squeak noise, used to lure them into close shooting range.

To hunt the rats I would sneak along the shore with Skipper at heal. Periodically I would place my forefinger over my lips and hold it in an arc pressing my lips lightly. I would suck in, making a squeaking noise. I would make a continuous set of squeaks for five to ten seconds, and then I would wait 15 or 20 seconds and repeat the procedure. It wouldn't be too long before a muskrat would swim to the noise, and I would shoot it in the head. The dog would then jump in and retrieve the rat.

As I stepped, putting weight down on my foot, the sod gave way. I crashed through the sod into a beaver run. I found myself up to my armpits in icy cold water. I thought, *What on earth am I going to do now?* I pulled myself out of the hole and hurried back to Joe's fire.

I could see the fire in the twilight of the night sky. It looked as though the whole island was ablaze. When I arrived, I saw he had a whole spruce tree on fire from one end to the other. I was surely glad since I was soaked. I peeled off my clothes and stretched out before the burning log. It felt good but only on the fire side. Meanwhile, my back side was getting cold. I kept turning like I was on a spit. I stuck branches into the muskeg and hung my wet clothes near the fire to dry. I maintained some comfort in the process, but always had a cold side exposed to the elements.

Joe took the rats and skewered and roasted them. He began to eat with relish. I laid hold of a skewered rat that looked done and began to eat, also. Not bad fare when you're cold, tired, naked, and starved. I thought to myself, *Naked I came into this world and naked I am, but I sure would be happy to have dry clothes on right now.*

It wasn't too long before my clothes were dry enough to wear so I could get on with the hunt. I said to Joe, "What I like about Alaska is that in the winter you don't have to contend with flying, biting bugs, and in the summer you aren't cold." Being a native Alaskan, I don't think he saw the humor in that remark, as it was just too true.

Eating Muskrat

Joe had several skewered muskrats roasted, and we ate when we felt like it and continued hunting through the night, taking a lot of muskrats. The next morning when it warmed, we lay down on one of the few dry spots next to the embers of the dying blaze Joe had set the night before.

We skinned the rats we had shot, and I packed as many of the pelts as I could in Skipper's pack. The rest of the pelts we each put in our individual packs. Joe gave a look of approval and said, "That is old Indian way. Roper, you make a good Indian."

We took a good long nap and slept very comfortably on the fire heated ground. When we woke, I took my New Testament out of my shirt pocket and read a passage of scripture for our devotions for the day. Joe and Elvin were both Christian believers so we prayed together. Then we set out for the river and our canoe. It was quite an experience to go with so little to carry. We certainly were unencumbered.

We went back across the river to a tributary coming into the river. I guided the canoe up the creek, which was running full. It took us to a lake where Joe had a family cabin, and we could stay overnight while we hunted the lake.

In the cabin were the makings for spaghetti without hamburger. We enjoyed the meatless pasta for a break from skewered muskrat. Our plan was to sleep by day and hunt by night.

That evening we took the canoe out on the lake and hunted for more rats, and in the process Joe killed a couple of beaver.

Bible study in the muskeg

Beaver are highly desirable fur animals and sought after by Indian trappers. They are the largest rodent in North America, weighing from 30 to 70 pounds. They breed during February and March under the ice and have three to four "kits."

This called for a change of menu. Now our evening meal was beaver, and it was tasty.

We hunted all night and the next day. In mid-afternoon we packed our furs, turned the canoe toward the river, and began the trip downstream to our vehicles.

On the way Elvin shot a large beaver that must have weighed at least 50 pounds. Skipper jumped into the raging current with no hesitation and grabbed the beaver. He turned toward shore and struggled to carry the beaver out of the river.

It was nearly an impossible task for him to fight against the current, which was pulling him downstream as he was trying to climb the nearly vertical bank about two feet above the water line. Knowing we wouldn't be able to get Skipper and his prize into the canoe without tipping over, we beached the canoe.

The family cabin

With determination, Skipper finally made it out and dragged the beaver over to me. A prouder dog you have never seen. He shook himself, covering us with a shower of water. Then he began to wriggle from head to tail and wag his otter-shaped tail. "Good dog," I said, and he seemed to be grinning. I bet he was thinking, *Hey, Dad, aren't you proud of me?*

I was sitting on the ground and Skipper just about turned himself inside out trying to sit his 90-pound frame on me. He was soaking wet and did a pretty good job of getting me just as wet. I praised him with enthusiasm that matched his. After all, he was the best dog on the river.

We got back into the canoe and continued down river to the vehicles. When we arrived, to my surprise, Betty and Laren were waiting. They thought we would be coming and were anxious to see us and find out how we had weathered the trip.

I think I was being tested by my Indian friends. They wanted to see if I had it in me to venture into the wilderness with so little in terms of camping gear and food.

I later learned I had passed the test when in church Joe came forward to tell his people about our trip. What had impressed him most was my taking time out to have devotions.

He said, "This man lives what he preaches." I thought, *We never know how our behavior is being read by those around us.* I prayed that I would be used to help these two men grow even more in their spiritual walk. This trip was a breakthrough in terms of sealing friendships.

I believe the Indian people were influenced more when we didn't have to talk but could just be there and let our actions do the talking. They say the average white man has a rubber tongue. One of my wife's complaints about me is that I don't talk enough. This may have been a plus in working with the Athabascan people.

On the way home Skipper was tired and perhaps chilled from lying in the bottom of the aluminum boat with near freezing water below. He went to sleep in the back of our van. He was really Laren's dog, so Laren crawled into the back to pet him.

When he touched the dog, Skipper must have thought he was being attacked or that he needed to protect the furs next to him. He snapped at Laren, biting him on the chin, tearing Laren's face from his lower lip to the bottom of his chin. Laren was in a lot of pain, so we drove the 50 miles to Faith Emergency Hospital in record time. We were pretty upset that Skipper had acted so aggressive.

The doctor sewed the flap of skin back into its original position. He made detailed, tiny stitches. It was an excellent job of sewing. In fact, Laren doesn't have any visible scar to remind us of the mishap.

Betty said, "We need to get rid of Skipper. I believe he's dangerous."

Laren heard us talking and, with tears running down his cheeks, said, "Please don't take Skipper away! I love him. Dad, you just can't take him to the dog shelter. They'll kill him, and it wasn't his fault!"

Laren's tears and heartfelt plea got to both Betty and me. Betty said, "We're just too emotional right now to make a good decision." I looked at Laren and Skipper. Laren's arm was around the dog's neck, and Skipper was panting, looking at us as if to say, *What's all the fuss about?*

We knew the dog had been in a deep sleep of exhaustion, and we could see how he might have been startled, giving a predictable survival reaction. I looked at Laren, who was shedding silent tears, and I said, "Son, your mom and I are really worried that Skipper might be getting vicious when he needs to protect his food. But we can see how this was an unusual situation, and we'll give him another chance. We know you really are buddies with him. We love him, too." So we agreed to keep Skipper. Relieved, wounded, and happy, Laren slept with Skipper that night. We knew we had made the right decision.

Looking back at the trip with Joe and Elvin, we could see the working of the Lord in every detail.

Chapter 10
License to Hunt

Betty and I were visiting with George and his wife Cheryl in their home. George and Cheryl were missionaries helping us in the Copper Center Chapel, a Native Indian chapel.

George had always wanted to hunt moose and also felt pressure to be successful so he wouldn't be classified as a "chechako," the Native term for a dude or tenderfoot. Unless you're a successful hunter, you are considered a chechako.

George and Cheryl were assigned to KCAM, an important Christian radio outreach in south-central Alaska. They lived in Glennallen and drove to Copper Center, 17 miles south on the Richardson Highway, to help in the Indian ministry.

George had never killed a moose, and we decided it was time to remedy that. We often talked about moose hunting, and George was always full of questions and had plenty of desire.

To add incentive to the hunt, Laren, our son, who was a quiet bystander at age twelve, spoke up and said, "Dad, I want to get a moose too. What about me?"

I said, "Yeah, you're old enough. It's time you and George both got a chance at a moose."

George had grown up in Minnesota and had never hunted or camped. However, he loved the outdoor environment and loved Alaska and wanted to expand his abilities. We planned an all-day moose hunt at 54 Mile Creek on the Valdez to Glennallen stretch of the Richardson Highway. I planned to take them to the same area where I had harvested my first Alaskan moose.

We arrived and parked at the 54 Mile pull-out, ready to go at daybreak.

Donning our day packs, we checked our equipment and began a steep three-mile climb to a bench above the timberline. We climbed and visited on rest stops, and we all had a keen anticipation for the day's hunt.

We were glad to have the privilege of being in such a beautiful setting. George exercised and ran consistently, so he was in good condition and was ready for the trail and rigors of moose hunting in rough country. I thought it strange that George had never hunted before, because he was right at home in this environment. I figured he would be a natural, but now it was time for action. We were in moose country and could see one at any time.

Larry's first Alaskan moose taken at 54 Mile, Richardson Highway

Just above timberline we traversed across the steep slope in a mixed shrub habitat. We were in a good position to see any moose moving throughout this zone. It was typical fall moose habitat. The mixed cover was made up of small patches of alders, a couple of species of willows, buffalo berry, high-bush cranberry, and small birch. We were sitting high above the bench scanning the brushy hillside below with field glasses. This was the same location where I had taken my first bull moose.

Seasoned hunters know the time spent sitting and glassing any area of good habitat is not time wasted. It is one of the best techniques to have increased opportunities and a successful hunt.

Usually after spotting a bull, we spend time letting him show us where he wants to be. We like to wait until the moose beds and then plan a sneak using the terrain and wind direction to dictate the route to take.

The temperature was a mild 50 degrees. The hillsides were brilliant with fall foliage turned to many of the russet browns, yellows, oranges, and deep reds typical of fall colors. It was as if the Lord took His palette and spread the colors in an arrangement. The colors varied from beautiful yellows to deep oranges, depending on the species. The birch was yellow while the buffalo berry was reddish-purple, and the alders were still green. The alders occurred in small copses on this east-facing slope, providing heavy cover interspersed with low brush.

While we were sitting at our observation post, Laren exclaimed with excitement in his voice, "Look, two big bulls are coming our way!" They were working their way from the west to the bench below. With adrenalin flowing freely in each of us, we waited to see where they were going.

George said, "Wow, those are nice bulls. In fact, they must be twins. They look just alike."

The two bulls had about 50-inch antler spreads with beautifully formed antlers. They were about 300 yards below to the south of us. Each bull searched around for a few minutes, apparently looking for just the right spot to bed down for their midday rest to chew their morning feed.

Even though we were excited, we checked the wind and took the time to plan our stalk. The last 25 yards required crawling behind a low hillock with high rye grass. Then we could ease up to the crest and look over the edge of the hill through the grass. We lay parallel to each other looking over the hill to see if the bulls were still there.

They were there, all right, at about 100 yards with shoulders exposed to us. I told Laren to get in place and to shoot as soon as George shot. Laren said he was too short and couldn't see over the grass. He said George should go ahead and take a bull, then he could stand up and maybe get a shot. I told George to aim right behind the shoulder and squeeze the trigger without a jerk.

Peering through the high rye grass, I said to George and Laren, "George, you shoot first, and Laren you shoot as soon after as you can. Let's see if we can get both of these bulls."

Laren said, "Dad, I'm just too short! I can't see over that grass at all."

I replied, "All right then, I'll shoot as soon as George shoots. Okay, George, get ready."

What was taking George so long? He should shoot! Those two bulls aren't going to wait all day! I thought sure he'd shoot when he got the crosshairs positioned behind the shoulder.

It seemed like it was taking forever. In reality it was about 25 to 30 seconds, but that's a long time when a game animal is about to take flight.

We waited and waited, and then waited some more. I could not understand why George didn't shoot. I was about to ask him what was wrong when the bulls jumped up as though they had caught our scent on a swirling breeze.

They started to run, and I took a shot at the nearest bull. He went to his knees. Then he got up, running to my left below an alder thicket. Now I was on automatic pilot, and without thinking, I jumped up and ran around the alder stand to the left. I knew full well that to go through the alders was nearly impossible. Something inside me took over. I was part of the environment, and like the lobo wolf, I was going in for the kill.

George, not knowing what it was like to try to get through an alder patch, ran a straight line toward the moose. He got so tangled in the alders, he never made it to the other side in time to see the bulls again. I was in the open, since I had run around the alders, and the bull I had hit was walking below me about 50 yards away. I put a quick shot behind his shoulder. He went down. We had one moose for sure.

George and Laren finally got through the brush, and I asked George why he hadn't shot. He said he had been perfectly lined up but had waited for me to tell him to shoot. I said, "Oh, I thought you'd shoot when you were ready. Neither Laren nor I were going to shoot until you did."

George was pretty bummed out over this but didn't say much. I felt bad that I hadn't communicated better. If I could hear George's mind working, I probably would've heard it struggling with negative versus positive thinking. We later discovered what was really going on, and George saw a higher reason for his hesitation to shoot.

George and Larry talk it over.

But, not knowing this reason, there was probably a battle going on inside George. The internal fight in a person's mind helps in coping with human error. At any rate, George appeared to have won the battle and accepted what had happened. It was pretty impressive, the way he handled our miscommunication. I had a suspicion that he was going to be a better hunter because of what had happened.

After the bull was skinned and boned, we packed as much as we could carry in one trip in our heavy duty Kelty backpacks. I took my tags out to punch the sex and date of kill, which showed the tags had been used.

George asked, "What are you doing?"

I said, "I'm punching out the date of kill and sex on the carcass tag." The moose tags were with my license, and according to game regulations, hunters are required to punch out the date of kill and sex of the animal upon taking it. "We can keep the tags on us until we're ready to transport the moose in our vehicles. Then the tags must be on the carcass to be legal."

"How did you get the moose tags?" George asked.

I said, "You ask for a moose permit when you buy your general license. The carcass tags are part of the moose permit or the permit for each game animal you want to hunt."

He looked shocked for a minute, and then he grinned like a light had just come on. "That must be why I didn't shoot. The Lord prevented me from shooting since I actually had no moose permit and was hunting illegally."

George had a strong sense of what was right and wrong. He stopped hunting for the rest of the trip, since he had only bought the general hunting license and had failed to obtain any specific tag for the big game animal he wanted to hunt. Now we understood why George was waiting to squeeze the trigger. In addition, George was careful, and it's so much better to hunt with a guy like George than with someone who is impulsive and trigger happy, who could care less about doing the right thing.

This was a tremendous witness to Laren and me. His doing what was right was far more important than being a successful hunter. In fact, this character trait made George a success regardless of whether or not he got a moose. He demonstrated the old axiom that "character is what you do when others aren't looking." We probably could have gotten away with putting my tags on the moose if George had of killed it, but we would have lost some integrity within ourselves had we done so.

We each struggled to put our packs on our backs. They weighed about 80 to 90 pounds. We started out through the brush on a moose trail.

Take your time and enjoy the packing

We had at least three and a half miles to pack down the mountain. One trip a day was all we'd be able to handle physically, since the trail was steep and difficult to climb or descend with heavy packs.

Because of the terrain, we decided to pack the rest of the moose the next day. We also thought it was a good idea to solicit some help for the rest of the job. George was a different man as we picked our way through the brush homeward bound. He had a song of joy in his heart.

We asked two of the men from the mission to help us and they were delighted. With four men packing, we were able to get all the meat out in one day. We shared the moose meat with everyone.

One man had arrived with his wife and children as new missionaries the week before we went on our hunt. This was his first outing in Alaska, and he was overjoyed to be asked to help.

Our other helper had never been in the mountains in road-less terrain before, as he was legally blind and people thought of him as a handicapped person not able to go into the wilderness. He was handicapped, but with guidance and patience, he could pack moose meat as well as anyone. He was grateful for being included and thought of as capable. We all enjoyed the fellowship even though it was hard labor.

Packing out of 54 Mile

George learned two valuable lessons that trip. The first was to be sure to get the correct license and tags for the species you plan to hunt. The second was to rely on yourself as to when to take your shot.

There were other lessons for all of us. For example, I learned that communication is the basis for building a friendship and helping each other have a successful hunt. I needed to be clear in communicating the details of buying a license as well as the actual shooting experience when I helped someone who had never hunted before.

Not everyone has the same skills in any endeavor. Perhaps the lessons were subtle. However, for a hunting neophyte, George learned to stalk with the wind blowing from the game animal to the hunter. He learned how to bone a moose, pack it out, and avoid hypothermia. In addition, he learned some hunting skills such as where to look for game and how to use your field glasses rather than hiking all over and possibly spooking the game before you have a chance to see it.

The greatest lesson we all learned was that God loves us and provides for us even when we're not aware of it. For me, the great outdoors is where I slow down enough to meditate and pray more. That is what I ought to be doing even when I'm not out in the field. But it's when I am out in nature that I take the time. I feel God's presence at these times, although I know He is constant and abides in me no matter where I am.

Character development occurs readily in the wilderness. Perhaps it's because of hardship, mistakes made, or by the fellowship of two or more working together to survive. We know that our character was tested on this short hunt, and it was honed for the future. It was a successful hunt.

Sharing the moose meat with three families

Chapter 11
Lung Infarction in the Back Country

"Son! I think I'm having a heart attack! Help me on my horse and let's get to camp as soon as possible. I have a pain in my chest that is excruciating."

Laren sprang into action, moving with the speed of lightning, and said, "Do you have any aspirin with you?"

"No, but I have these nitro tablets Mom insisted I bring with me." Laren directed me to take one. I did and we were on our way back to camp.

Betty had had a heart attack a few years earlier. As a result, she knew an infarction can occur suddenly and without warning. I'd had some signs of angina prior to our hunting trip but hadn't seen a doctor yet. Her insistence that I take a few of her nitro stat pills was insightful and may have saved my life.

We were camped in Patterson Creek in the Flattops Wilderness Area on the White River National Forest near Gypsum, Colorado.

Heading into Patterson Creek

For a lot of years I'd wanted to hunt the Patterson Creek drainage. At last my dream was to come true. The area had a reputation of being home to a large elk herd. When I was working for the U.S. Forest Service as a wildlife biologist and range conservationist, I had worked all around the canyon area of Patterson Creek but had never been able to actually get into the creek to get to know it firsthand.

Elk have been mythical creatures. "Grey ghosts," I call 'em.

We were camping just inside the Flat Tops Wilderness Boundary where we could drive a four-wheel pickup to the campsite and bring our saddle horses in by another shorter route. To drive to the campsite from the maintained road on a four-wheel-drive trail was about 11 miles, and to ride horseback on the Forest Service designated horse trail was about eight miles.

Our hunting crew this year was my friend Bill from Denver, his co-worker and friend, Steve, my son-in-law Randy, and my son Laren.

Bill and Steve were going to drive my pickup in on the four-wheel-drive trail while I was going to bring four horses via the eight-mile trail that pack stock and livestock used. Laren and Randy would come in their Chevy Blazer later that evening. Of the five of us, Bill was the only one familiar with the area and knew both the horse trail and the four-wheel-drive trail.

I had the tent and grub on the pack horses and planned on setting up the camp before the others arrived. In dry weather the trail would have been hard going, but the weather turned and it was snowing in earnest by late afternoon, making north central Colorado roads treacherous. I arrived at the campsite where the two trails converged. Bill had drawn me a map and explained where to set the camp.

A secure camp ready for the hunters

Same camp after a heavy snow

Using a lariat and my horse, I started dragging firewood to the chosen campsite. I would get off and put the loop of the lariat on the big end of the log or several logs, then mount and snake them in like a cowboy dragging calves to the branding fire.

Next I set up the tent, picketed the horses, and started a fire. I was glad to get those chores done before the snow began to accumulate in earnest. Being alone and the weather threatening a blizzard were added incentives to get a lot of wood into camp.

Larry wonders if Steve and Bill have broke down.

Bill and Steve were long overdue. I got nervous and had a hunch they were in trouble. I saddled my stallion, Rhythm, and rode back down the four-wheel-drive trail looking for them. The wind was picking up and the snow was getting deeper. About five inches had accumulated. About two miles back up the four-wheel-drive trail I found Bill and Steve high centered on a rock.

My extra hand was just what was needed. We got the pickup off the rock, and they drove ahead of me to arrive at camp with plenty of time to get unpacked.

Everybody worked and we had a cozy camp established before dark. Laren and Randy should have arrived by the time we ate supper. The snow was now about ten to twelve inches deep and they still had not arrived.

I was really uneasy. I said, "Those boys have no business driving in on the Jeep trail after dark in this snow storm.

Steve looked at me with grave concern showing on his face. "I'm worried about the boys, too."

Larry decided he better go look for Bill and Steve

The wind had stopped but the snow was coming down in big, soft flakes. Talking it over, we decided that since it was well after dark, it would be too dangerous for Laren and Randy to attempt to drive in the 11 miles.

I said, "I think I'll ride out on horseback to find them and stay all night where we left the horse trailer. Then we'll come in tomorrow since it's the opening day of elk season and hunt on the way in on the horse trail."

They agreed, so I saddled up Baby Dawn, our gray mare that was trail wise and would not get lost. She had proven to us many times that she could find her way to camp in the blackest night conditions.

It was still snowing hard, and I could just make out the tops of the trees in the falling snow and the darkness. If it hadn't been such an urgent, anxiety-filled trip, I could have really enjoyed the ride out.

It was beautiful. I looked up into the sky, and the snowflakes were about the size of 50-cent coins. They would hit my cheeks and for a few moments they would not melt. The treetops were silhouetted against the snow-filled sky, and I felt the clopping of the horse's feet as she shuffled through the snow.

I let Baby Dawn find her own way and trusted she would stay on the trail. The trail wound through patches of timber and in and out of open, park-like meadows. The ride was pretty dangerous as I couldn't tell whether or not we were on the trail. I had a foreboding that something was wrong.

About midnight my horse stopped and did not want to go. "Come on, Baby Dawn," I said. "Don't be a quitter on me." It was so dark I wasn't sure where we were. I rode around in a small circle and nearly bumped into the trailer. That's why the mare had stopped and wouldn't continue. We had made it to the trailer and Bill's parked vehicle.

I was soaked from the heavy, wet snow and was beginning to get extremely cold. I grained the mare and picketed her in some good grass along the creek bottom. In order to feed, the horse had to paw away the snow to eat the abundant meadow grass. Looking around, I could see that Laren and Randy were not there.

I knew I needed shelter, warmth, and dry clothes. I couldn't do anything for Laren and Randy until daybreak. In fact, I would be in a world of hurt if I didn't find a way to have some sort of shelter. I explored and discovered a big tent not too far from the trailer. It turned out to be a cook tent for about eight to ten hunters from Arkansas. I woke them and explained my predicament. They were "good old boys" and let me stay the night in their cook tent.

I built up the fire, took off my wet clothes, and hung them near the stove to dry. I slept in an extra sleeping bag the hunters loaned me. If I hadn't found these Arkansas hunters, I would have been in a life-threatening situation.

The hunters woke me around 5 a.m. when they came into the cook tent to eat and get ready to hunt. They graciously fed me breakfast. The hunters were from Arkansas farm country and had a "country" hospitality outlook on life. They loved to hunt and valued helping their fellow man.

I thought, *No matter what you may have heard about non-resident hunters, these fellows exhibited true southern hospitality. These guys have just proven to me it is the real deal. I will always be grateful to a bunch of guys I really did not know. They're top notch in my book.*

They loaned me a four-wheel-drive Bronco to go down the mountain main access road to look for my boys. I drove about eight to ten miles down the road and found them walking up the road. They were in good spirits after having spent the night sleeping in the seats of their Blazer. The snow was about a foot deep at the lower elevation where the old Blazer had quit running with transmission problems. I was sure glad to see them and told them how far they had yet to go. They were thankful I had come looking for them.

We gathered their gear, left the Blazer where it was, and went back to the Arkansas hunters' camp. I loaded Baby Dawn with Laren and Randy's outfit, and we walked in the eight miles on the horse trail. The snow was about 16 to 20 inches deep and it was not easy going.

At camp we took a short rest and decided to go for an evening hunt. Laren and I decided to hunt together. We took the stud horse and started down the Patterson Creek trail. It was steep but good going and excellent elk habitat.

We were walking along, moving from lookout to lookout, when I experienced sudden intense pain in my chest. It was so severe I called to Laren, who wasn't far away. I had some nitro stat pills Betty insisted I keep with me. I put one tablet under my tongue and waited five minutes, then I took another nitro pill. The pain continued so I took the third pill. After the third pill and still no relief of pain, I said, "Let's get back to camp as soon as possible." I was really alarmed!

Laren gets ready to help his dad get back to camp.

By the time we got to camp, I knew my condition was extremely serious and I should be in a hospital. The other guys hadn't come in yet from hunting, so I took some aspirin and went to bed.

Extreme back pain, chills, and aches were telling me I was having a heart attack or something similar. I knew I was in deep trouble. I hated to ruin everybody's hunting trip, but knew I needed a doctor. We were about 10,000 feet above sea level, and I was in bed with chest pain. We were 30 to 40 miles from the nearest hospital, with 18 inches of snow on the ground. These conditions made my medical situation critical.

When the hunters returned, we all concluded I should be in the hospital. I was in a near fatal situation. I told the guys, "This may be it. I may not be going home to my wife. I'd really like to stay on this old earth and be what I can be for my family. I don't believe Betty should be left alone." I prayed, "Lord, deliver all of us guys from the hand of the wilderness. I know the wilderness is impartial and only takes those who are unable to cope. Lord, we have done everything we could to have a good hunt and be safe, honoring You in the way we camp and hunt. Now You are our lifeline."

I had to give up on my dream for this year.

Laren and Bill chained the tires on the pickup all the way around as we were concerned that we might not make it out, considering the snow depth and trail conditions.

It was a perilous drive. It was rough, and I wondered again if I was going to make it out alive. The pain in my chest was excruciating. Bill did a good job of driving and kept from getting stuck or hung up on any rocks, but the going was slow. Finally, we made it to the main road off the Flat Tops and drove through Dotsero and onto Interstate 70. We drove through the Glenwood Canyon to the Glenwood Springs Hospital. It was truly a miracle to arrive and still be alive.

Tests in the emergency room revealed I was not having a heart attack. The doctors were stumped but did get the pain under control. However, after three weeks and two different hospitalizations, we learned I had a lung infarction caused by a blood clot in my left lung. The doctors also discovered I had two blocked main arteries to my heart. In other words, I was set up for a heart attack.

I learned a lot from the Patterson Creek elk hunt. Mainly, I realized that I tried to do too much by myself. I had needed at least one other man with me to help in the extreme weather conditions. When going into strange country, it's best to go with someone who knows the area rather than go in alone. Furthermore, I learned the value of having basic medical supplies in camp.

The trip also reinforced things we did correctly. We had extra firewood cut ahead of time, and our horses were well trained and dependable mountain horses. We had survival gear and planned the trip well, knowing we needed to be prepared for extremes in the weather. As usual, we had set up the tents so that they would bear the weight of the snow. Even so, we had to stay vigilant and beat the snow off as it fell.

Most of all, we recognized when to call it quits and submit to the need for seeing a doctor, even if it meant no elk hunting. We were in a tight situation but used our ingenuity and resources to avoid a potential tragedy.

Chapter 12

Christian Fellowship in Hell's Hole

We were waiting in the back yard of our home on Gore Pass for Bill and his friend Steve to arrive. Bill was from Denver and had hunted elk with me several years. As usual, he used the time out hunting as a platform to bring someone he either was discipling or wanted to lead to the Lord. This year he brought Steve, a friend and co-worker. Steve's parents were former missionaries from Brazil. He was raised in Brazil and had many stories to tell. In addition to that résumé, he had been the UCLA soccer coach.

While we were waiting, I thought back to all the guys who've have made Hell's Hole their fall hunting camp home with us. It has been a privilege to share these experiences and provide horses and camp for my friends and relatives.

In Hell's Hole camp

My brother-in-law Gary and his son David have been with us numerous times. This particular year they wouldn't make it but I'd tell the new guys about them and show where they'd gotten their elk.

Waiting should've been easy enough, but I'm always anxious to get packed into elk camp as early as possible. It's not so easy when you remember all the good times.

139

The aspens were in golden array, and we were poised for the first big snow of the season to blanket us. All signs signaled that winter was just around the corner. However, this day was perfection and could not be any better even if we had ordered it special delivery.

We're anxiously awaiting the arrival of Bill and Steve so we can pack into Hell's Hole. Larry and Randy are getting saddle gear ready at the coral. Josh and Dan are on horses. Betty and her friend chit-chat.

Randy, my son-in-law, was taking his two boys, our grandsons—Josh, age 13, and Dan, age 11—into camp with us. They were going to Hell's Hole to fish rather than hunt. Troublesome Creek was their objective. Hunting elk would come later in their lives, but for the present, they were bent on fishing while we hunted. They were as excited as if they were selected to go to the moon.

These two grandsons of ours were truly dyed-in-the-wool fishermen. They were adept, having a special gift in their ability to nab a skittish trout in a crystal clear trout stream.

"I bet I catch the biggest fish," said Josh, but Dan came right back with, "Maybe so, but I bet I catch the most. I'm going to feed the whole camp the best German browns they've ever eaten." The boys were competitive and were driven to be all they could be as fishermen, and they simply loved to be in the back country.

Our personal gear, the general camp gear, and groceries were organized in like stacks ready to be stowed in the panniers. The horses were ready to load into the trailers, and there was excitement in the air along with the anticipation of the unknown.

It was a bluebird day of Indian summer. We all know those days when the sun warms up and summer has returned for one last fling before old man winter arrives for the season.

Mother Nature was just fooling, because the nights were near freezing and the nighttime temperatures along with the crisp bite in the air let us know we had better be prepared for winter. However, the daytime temperatures and the clear blue sky gave us a perfect day for the start of the fall hunt to get our meat for the year. You might say Indian summer is the lull before the storm.

At last the tardy hunters drove into the yard, and we added their gear to the piles of hobbles, ropes, axes, lanterns, stove, knives, whetstones, etc., that we had laid out. To look at the piles of gear, one would think that it would be impossible to get all of it on just four horses.

We had four pack horses and four riding horses. There were four men and two boys. The boys were up for walking into our elk camp, which was about a three-mile trek from the road on top of Black Mountain. Going in, the trail wound through the trees around the rim of Hell's Hole about a mile-and-a-half and then dropped steeply into the Hole for the next mile or two.

Our campsite was about two miles above Troublesome Creek and was in a road-less area. Through the years we had noticed that it was an area that branch-antlered bulls seemed to prefer. In other adjacent areas we would see younger bulls, but we'd often see large numbers of cows and calves with them. But Hell's Hole seemed to produce a more even ratio of cows to larger bulls. This is probably because of light hunting pressure compared to surrounding, more accessible areas.

After introductions and a short time of small talk, we separated the gear into reasonable packs for each horse. One of the keys to successful horse packing was to have the panniers balanced in weight. A packer needs to be particular about this, and the fellows caught on right away to just how important it was.

To everyone's surprise, we fit everything into four packs and didn't have to leave anything. It was still early in the morning and the day before the season opened. We loaded up and kissed our wives and kids goodbye.

On the way up Black Mountain, I told the men more about Hell's Hole. "It's about 10,000 feet elevation around the rim, and our camp is at about 8,500 feet above sea level. Every trail from camp is a happy climb either up or down. There is no such thing as flat in this country. It takes two things to get along in here. You better have great legs and fantastic lungs." I laughed and added, "Plus, you better have tremendous desire or the Hole will beat you up."

I continued with my explanation. "It'll take us another 45 minutes on the four-wheel drive trail to the top of Black Mountain where we'll unload the horses, saddle up, and pack each horse. I'll tie the final double diamond hitch on each pack to be sure we don't lose a load on the way in. In the process of packing through the week, I'll show each of you guys how to tie a double diamond hitch so we can all share the work involved in packing."

Since the panniers were packed before we left our house, all we had to do was unload the horses and gear, saddle each horse, then load the packs and tie the traditional double diamond hitch. This ensured each pack would make the trip through trees over logs and down steep inclines.

It sounds simple and relatively safe. We started packing the horses, and as I finished the diamond hitch on the horse I called Rhythm, something spooked him and he blew up. He set back on the tie rope, but he had been trained to give to pressure, so he lunged forward and the pack hit the tree he was tied to and threw him off balance, causing him to fall.

He had solid plywood panniers packed full of our groceries. I needed help. I yelled, "Hey, I need some help! This doggone horse just blew up as I finished the hitch."

Randy came running over and exclaimed, "What on earth happened? I haven't ever seen the like."

There on the ground with his halter rope stretched tight, tied to a big lodgepole pine, was Rythm. He was upside down, scrunched between two kitchen pannier boxes and not even moving.

A mild insurrection

I remembered in Joe Back's book, *Horses, Hitches and Rocky Trails*, he called something like this a "mild insurrection." Randy helped me unpack Rhythm, stand him up, and re-pack him. No problem! "Whew! Murphy's law still is viable," I exclaimed. "If anything can go wrong, IT WILL! In this case, it sure did."

At last we are ready to ride.

The horse wasn't hurt, I wasn't hurt, and both the horse and I were much smarter than we were before it happened. The result was a much calmer, more well-mannered horse who would stand still.

At last we were mounted and rode down the trail with each rider leading a pack horse. The boys ran ahead or lagged behind and were running off pent up energy.

I can still smell the balmy, heavy scent of the sub-alpine fir as we rode through the forest. I can close my eyes and hear the saddles creaking and ocassionally hear a top pack scrape against a limb as a horse slid down an incline in the trail and came in contact with a low limb. All these incidents, sights, sounds, and smells encountered in a wilderness pack trip are embedded in my brain forever. All I have to do is close my eyes and picture the scenes, and it all comes back to me.

Once in a while we had problems with a pack either catching the hitch rope on a limb or a saddle turning sideways. We were about halfway to our campsite when Beauty caught her rope on a stout limb. The guys took a rest break while they watched Randy and me straighten the saddle and re-tie the pack.

A tie rope caught a limb.

The trip in was beautiful, and except for two problems with a couple of horses, it was for all practical purposes uneventful. The terrain was rough with a lot of timber, and there was always a chance of a horse getting on the wrong side of a tree or getting his pack rope caught under the tail of the horse in front of him. After a horse has packed a few loads through the timber, he will rarely hit a tree as he knows just how much space he needs to get through the forest. He also won't come unglued when a rope does get under his tail.

One of the drawing cards for going into the Hole to hunt was the fact that the surrounding areas had access for hunters with four-wheel drive pickups. However, there was no way to get into the Hole with a vehicle, and not many hunters were inclined to kill an elk deep in the Hole knowing the steep terrain would nearly preclude getting an elk out without a horse to pack it.

In camp and waiting for the opening day tomorrow

We arrived at the campsite and set up our tents, hobbled the horses, and got ready to hunt. I had come in the weekend before and cut up enough firewood to last for an eight- to ten-day hunt. The camp was at the head of a beautiful mountain meadow with a spring feeding a small stream that bubbled musically along just below the tents.

Finally, we had time to light a campfire, as all the camp chores were pretty well in hand. The lanterns were gassed, wood was stacked in the tent behind the sheep herder's stove, and a fire was going in the stove. The little sheet metal stove was beginning to put out a lot of heat. This was the same stove my dad had used when I was a kid. It was handed down to me and is one of my prized possessions. Its unique design included an oven that biscuits could be made in, and it could be packed easily between the two panniers across the saddle perpendicular to the pack saddle.

Our bedrolls were rolled out and we were ready. Randy, the boys, and I were sleeping in a 10 x 12-foot wall tent. Our tent doubled as the cook tent and gathering place for evening storytelling and devotional reading. Bill and Steve were in a sleeping tent nearby.

Bill started the evening off with devotions. He read a scripture verse or two. We talked about it and how it applied to our lives and our hunting trip.

We were crowded in the tent but enjoyed the fellowship as we got better acquainted. Stories began to flow, and we pulled out the map of the area to acquaint Steve with the locations where we had killed elk in the past. Each kill site was marked on the topographic map, and you could definitely see a pattern.

We believed that if elk were there before, then the likelihood was high for them to be there again. I asked where each man wanted to hunt. Randy knew exactly where he wanted to go as he had hunted the Hole with me for several years. He was exceptionally skilled at finding game and had been successful through the years we hunted together.

Steve only had three days to hunt as he had to return to Denver for work. We decided to hunt together since Steve didn't know the area and had the least time to hunt, and I knew the area quite well.

The next morning I woke early and got the fire going in the stove. "All right, you guys, up and at 'em! I'll bring the horses in and get them grained and saddled. Do you suppose you guys could get breakfast ready and lunches made for each of us?"

All the morning chores were done in a speedy manner and everyone helped. It was just cracking dawn when we hit the saddles and started down the trail toward the Troublesome. Frost was in the air, and the horses had rattles in their noses, snorting and blowing as they warmed up to the task.

About a half mile from camp some deer crossed our trail in front of us. The horses spotted them before we did, and we watched them as they filed across perpendicular to our route of travel. As we rode down to the creek I said, "Keep a sharp eye out for elk on the sagebrush hillside to our right. I've seen them grazing more than once on that hillside."

We often got a deer in the area if we had both a deer and an elk license.

Hell's Hole was an example of excellent elk habitat. It had edges of timber for cover adjacent to feed areas with plenty of water. Biologists use the term "juxtaposition" to describe the quality of the habitat. This area had good juxtaposition. That is, the ratio of cover to feed areas and available water was just right.

It was the habit of the elk to bed down at the head of the draws in heavy timber. Early in the morning they would file out and down a trail from the forest to the crest of the ridge. They would gradually graze into the sagebrush hillside before going back into the timber later in the morning. Their route would usually take them to running water as they moved into their bedding areas.

A series of deep ravines parallel to each other drained from the main high ridge to the south. Troublesome Creek meandered in a northwesterly direction and in general ran from the east to the west. The terrain on the north side of the creek had a southern exposure and was primarily sagebrush. There were several deep draws running from north to south cutting up that side of the drainage. Higher up on the north side of the creek the lodgepole pine covered the mountain, and it also contained good numbers of elk and deer.

Bill and Randy were going to hunt the north side of the drainage, and Steve and I would hunt the south side. We would climb to the main timbered ridge and then hunt down spur ridges back towards the Troublesome. We could sit on one of the spur ridges and watch one of the many trails that contoured from the pines around to the open sagebrush into the draw.

Steve and I left Randy and Bill at the creek crossing. Before we got out of the water, the horse Steve was riding began to lunge around for what appeared to be no good reason.

However, there is always a reason. Sometimes we humans don't know what it is, but horses are prey animals, and much of their behavior is in response to what they perceive as danger. Steve might have been holding the reins too tight or giving some subtle signal to his horse. He yelled, "What should I do?" Then he lost his balance and fell into a pool of water about two feet deep.

"Boy! This is cold!" exclaimed Steve. We had a good laugh, but we also knew the gravity of the situation.

I said, "The first rule of getting bucked off is to get back on."

"Okay, but how do I know she won't do it again?"

I answered, "You don't know, but you better get out of the water, and getting back on is the best way."

Fortunately, Steve was wearing waterproof duck hunting clothes and didn't get too wet. It was funny but also downright dangerous. Steve managed to get up and back on his horse which, ironically, was named Angel. She was not living up to her name at all.

Steve's good sense of humor returned. Later in camp we told the story with great embellishment. So we continued our hunt and rode into the mouth of the third draw east of our camp and began to climb to the top of the ridge.

The horses were blowing hard from the exertion of the climb. We stopped to let them air up. We looked up, and at the edge of the timber we saw several elk. In the foggy, dim dawn they looked like gray ghosts. They were too far for a shot, so we just watched as they moved into the timber.

"Let's let them go," I said. "They're headed towards a crossing from the timber to the sagebrush about a half mile south of us. There's a good elk trail coming out of the timber. We can wait for them out of sight, and then we can ease up to the edge of the timber and catch them as they cross the saddle."

We rode to the top of the ridge, tied the horses, then proceeded on foot. The ridge was a bench and was nearly level to the saddle where the elk would cross. Steve went on ahead and I came along about 75 yards behind. Musing to myself, I thought, *Steve's lack of experience in hunting elk and his novice horsemanship are teaching him on the fast track.* I grinned, realizing this was much more than an elk hunt for Steve. It was his first elk hunt.

"Okay," Steve said, thinking out loud. "Now I can be one on one with the elk. It is the hunter versus the hunted. The hunter must eat. The elk must live."

All of their senses were on alert. In fact, both elk and man lived on alert, for it was an age-old predator/prey relationship. Steve was the hunter and was now transformed in his re-enactment of our historical past. He was as primitive as the first cave man with a club and a flint point on a spear. He moved carefully, testing the wind.

I was moving as slowly and quietly as possible on the edge of the timber so I could look down the slope to the west. I had stopped to look and listen when I heard Steve shoot and then shoot again and again. I hurried to see what had happened and saw Steve standing and looking at the trail that crossed the saddle. "I missed," he said. That was a tough moment for Steve. He could not believe he could miss an elk standing broadside at about 70 yards.

I assured Steve that all hunters have had similar experiences. Steve said, "I must have had elk fever and clutched."

I agreed, and I said, "Your adrenalin push wasn't under control, and the fact that a nice five-point bull was standing broadside made it worse."

We hunted hard the rest of the day and the next. A better sport than Steve could not be found. In fact, Steve was grateful for the opportunity and was not despondent about missing a shot that should have been meat in the bag. In spite of the lost five-point bull, which had to be placed on the back burner and not dwelt upon, we looked around and realized what was really important to us.

Steve said, "For me to be able to relive a moment in history much the way our forbearers would have experienced, missing a game animal and having to go hungry another day was a great personal experience." He also recognized that the fellowship and companionship we all had developed was far more valuable than getting an elk.

A great way to hunt

In the meantime, the boys were keeping us in fish from their fishing ventures. It was great to have two young fishermen in camp. They had some nice brown trout, and they were bubbling with enthusiasm. They provided us with the best suppers you can imagine. The evening of the first day we had brown trout furnished by the boys.

We told stories, then hit the sack and looked forward to another day of hunting. Steve's stories of his growing up in South America were especially entertaining.

Overnight about six inches of snow fell, and Steve and I decided to hunt the slope east of the camp. We had often seen elk using the open sagebrush at the head of the draw where we camped.

We had been on our lookout since daybreak, and it was about 9 a.m. I was looking at the plume of smoke drifting skyward from our cook tent when the flap was thrown back and the two boys emerged. They rigged up their poles and took off down the trail to the Troublesome. They were in a school no man could duplicate. The subject was self-reliance in a wilderness environment.

Larry makes his way to the elk stand.

Later that day, around 3 p.m., Steve and I were back on our stand. We saw some movement coming up the trail below the camp. It was both boys again in the same frame as they were in the morning. They were dragging fish as they plodded up the trail. If I live to be a century old, I will never get that picture out of my mind. What made it so great was that we had three generations carrying on the tradition of hunting and, in this case, fishing for our food.

As I contemplated the scene, another picture came to my mind. This was a conjured up picture, drawn in my mind from the many times that I heard the story of the Roper boys' Model 1886 Winchester, caliber 40-82. It was a black powder lever action rifle with an octagonal barrel. Several of the Ropers were living in Victor, Colorado. It was at the height of the gold rush days. Among them were my Grandpa Tom and my Uncle Earl.

Apparently they had a tradition of making an annual trek using a team of horses pulling a draft wagon to the Piceance Creek basin to hunt for mule deer. One rifle is all they had, and the four or five brothers shared in the harvest. When they got the wagon full, they made the trip back through Leadville, Fairplay, and on to Victor. This was at least a 90- to 100-mile haul.

Dan and Josh learned early.

I wonder how many brothers could share one rifle and feed their families as a result of their combined cooperation. Perhaps Josh and Dan were walking in the same footsteps as their ancestors, the Roper boys.

Monday came all too soon, and I helped Steve pack his gear and ride out to the vehicles. I rode back into the camp and set out to hunt for the rest of the day. I thought about the events of the past two days and how the Lord had been the center of fellowship in the camp. God was close to us, and we asked Him to keep us safe and guide our way.

The hunt was a success, and we must not forget that when the Lord is put in first place, the outcome of the trip is always and will always be what each of us needs for further growth. We all learned from each other a valuable spinoff from hunting in a manner that took us back to the roots of human history.

Then I thought about Randy and what a great dad he was. He was there for Joshua and Daniel all their growing up years. He fished with them, hunted with them, and played ball and rough-housed with them. I have seen them grow up to be fine men with high values.

Bill brought with him the values of honesty and dedication to the Lord. He was always sharing in the work around the camp and ready to bring devotions to us in a way that was a blessing. Through the years we have had a lot of different men in the camp to hunt elk. Each has brought something of value to the Hole.

I determined to keep a sensible sense of humor and put disappointment in my pocket and keep it there. I hope one of the values I brought to the camp was that persistence pays off. Never give up, and if the season closes and you have not scored, just wait for next year. You'll get 'em with renewed vigor.

Persistence pays off.

We had meat to pack out.

Packing out our meat and trophies

True Camaraderie
By Larry Roper

It was evening and light was fading fast.
The birds were singing their evening song; daylight would not
      last.
The sky was red with hints of purple; even this would soon be
      over.
I watched the embers of our campfire, my thoughts as deep as
      a field of clover.

I wondered what the morrow would bring.
Now all was quiet, not a bird would sing.
The night air had a chill that penetrated deep.
It was time to hit the sack, for my thoughts would keep.

Visions of bugling bull elk were in my head.
Sleep was not an option, even though I was abed...
My stomach was atwitter as I planned the hunt in detail.
Would the night ever end so we could hit the trail?

Somehow I drifted off to sleep.
Suddenly I sat up straight, wide awake.
It was four bells, and my buddy was snoring deep.
I stirred the coals, lit the lantern, knowing sleep time would keep.

Wake up, wake up, my friend, it's on the mountain where elk do
      abide.
I'll fry some eggs and bacon while you dress,
Then I will catch the ponies and get them ready to ride.
Hurry, up and at 'em, for this is no game of chess.

It wasn't long and chores were done.
We saddled up with purpose as though we were one.
The horses had rattles in their nose,
And their foggy breath floated past our mounted toes.

We rode down into Hell's Hole,

Knowing where elk could be found.
Our horses stopped for water and made a slurping sound.
Daylight was approaching, and a browsing elk was our goal.

Up the hill the way was steep, and faint the trail as we took our
time.
At intervals we let the horses air up, for they labored in their
climb.
At each stop we did search for an elk above.
We knew we were close to our quarry provided by God's great
love.

Aha, there, the gray ghost moved to the ridge beyond our view.
It was a young bull on his way to the meadow that we knew.
If we circled around we would not be seen,
And then my partner could get a shot to complete his hunting
dream.

Our plan would work, we were absolutely sure.
We sneaked to the foot of an ol' limber pine,
Then we saw antler tips just below the horizon line.
His body came into view; his antlers they did lure.

The wind was right and the elk had no clue.
Wait, don't shoot, another bull came into view.
He stopped to look as elk often do.
Now Instead of one, we could have two.

The rest of the story is history; he shot and missed his aim.
Now we had nothing but a memory for a trophy to claim.
We returned to camp; the hunt was over and we must pack out.
We'll take our time, for in Hell's Hole it's best to go slow, without a
doubt.

You may wonder why this verse—what is the moral of this tale?
Could it be to teach us to enjoy the hunt's detail?
Remember such things as a horse's foggy breath, while on your
     mount,
Or enjoy eggs cooked on the fire, and cherish the friendship, for
     it does count.

Take what is, as nature gives; it is the Lord's gift to us,
And if you cannot sleep, it is best to adjust, but not a must.
Give God the credit for all opportunity,
Knowing fellowship with friends will last for eternity.

The hunt itself is an avenue
To bring us closer to God and friends like you.
It gives us a glimpse of His love so true.
It is life's simple way of letting God guide us through.

We will learn that success will come to us when we persevere.
Missing a shot is not the end; we have learned to be of good
     cheer.
Another day will come, and God will provide without fail.
We will come again to the Hole and take up another bull elk
     trail.

Chapter 13
Challenges

"Laren, hand me the camera. That's a beautiful sunset."

With panic written upon his face, 12-year-old Laren answered, "Dad, I lost the camera."

"You what? Son, how could you lose the camera? You hung it around your neck, didn't you?"

At first I thought this was terrible. How could we find such a small object in the middle of a wilderness? I looked at Laren's face, and knew I needed to handle this just right. I said, "We'll find it, don't worry."

We had stopped to catch our breath at the top of the steep climb. We were awed by the beauty and magnificence of the sunset and the Wrangell Mountains. We stood high above Copper Lake and south of the Nabesna River in a scene of splendor. It was incomparable to any sunset we had ever seen.

We were heavily loaded with sheep meat, cape, and horns, as well as a small bull caribou that Kristi, our 16-year-old daughter, had taken on the way in to find a Dall sheep. We set our packs down and took in the beauty. Turning to Laren, I said, "Anyone could have done the same thing. This country is tough on people and equipment."

Quickly, we went over the details. We rehashed the route we had taken from the sheep kill and realized the camera must be in the middle of the talus rockslide (a field of rocks of about ten acres and very steep). We had sat down for our first rest in this rock strewn slope on the way back to camp. There were only about 30 to 45 minutes of daylight left. I took my pack off and said, "You kids wait right here. I'll go back and find it." We haven't come very far. The fact was, the rock slide was only ten to fifteen minutes away if I hurried—and I could hurry.

Laren said, "Oh, Dad, you can't find it! It'll be like looking for a needle in a haystack."

I said, "Well, that may be so, but I believe if we ask the Lord to help us, we have a chance."

The day had been full of troubles as well as rewards as we neared the end of seven hard but wonderful days in the Wrangell Mountains in the interior of Alaska.

Two of our kids, Kristi and Laren, and Kristi's 17-year-old boyfriend Randy and I had decided to go sheep and caribou hunting. Meanwhile, Betty, my wife, was visiting her sister in California and our 14-year-old daughter Lori was working in Glennallen at the Tastee Freeze.

The trip had started off with great success. Laren was the first to score. He took a young caribou bull the first day not far from the road before we packed our base camp into the Wrangell Mountains near the headwaters of the Copper River. It was his first big game animal, and he made an excellent lung shot with his 30'06.

All our kids started shooting big game rifles with reduced loads in the heavier calibers. This meant less flinching from anticipated recoil. For Laren, we used a 150-grain Nosler bullet ahead of a powder that produced respectable velocity of about 2,700 feet per second, about 300 feet per second slower than a factory round. This reduced velocity controlled excessive recoil, yet would still pack a punch capable of bringing down a bear if needed.

Our destination was to set up base camp about 11 or 12 miles from the Nabesna road. Kristi and her boyfriend Randy were up for the challenge of a wilderness hunt with Laren, Jr., and me.

We were looking for a good wilderness experience and were hoping to fill at least one freezer with a winter's supply of meat. This was important because culturally in the Indian village the people shared meat, especially among the elderly. We wanted to be a part of that sharing.

This was one way we could fit in and be a part of the Indian community. Moose and caribou in particular are a part of the traditional cultural mindset. The sharing of game was especially important in the celebration of funeral rituals known as "potlatches." The potlatch is a cultural event used primarily to help the grieving process when a loved one dies. A simple explanation of a complex cultural event is difficult.

158

Athabascan men at a potlatch

Singing and dancing at a potlatch traditional funeral

Essentially, the potlatch is held in the home village of the closest relatives of the deceased. The potlatch begins with the funeral and lasts up to three or four days. The clan of the lost person hosts all other clans and feeds them and provides a place for them to stay. This keeps the grieving ones occupied serving others and having a purpose. It is a way of saying thank you for caring and coming to help us grieve.

At the end of the days of dancing, singing, and telling stories, performed by the visiting clans, gifts are brought out by the grieving clan members. Gifts are usually rifles, blankets, and Indian made traditional clothing. Other gifts could be knives, artwork, traps, sleds, or other articles traditionally used to survive. These gifts are given by the grief stricken families to the guests from surrounding areas and villages.

Gifts are given in a hierarchy of importance honoring the elderly first. Gifts are also given to regain peace between two individuals having "bad blood," or what we would classify as "relationship problems." If you are gifted by an enemy, then you will have peace. These celebrations are meaningful and religious and help preserve the culture.

Hunting is a vital part of the Athabascan culture. Moose and caribou are high on the list for potlatches. Hunting caribou is chancy since caribou are unpredictable in their movements in any given year. They are predictable over time, tending to travel on their migration routes year after year. If we could help provide some wild game meat for these events, we would be helping in a big way.

The timing of migration and the exact routes they take seem to be known only to the caribou. They can get up and go and travel great distances, and they tend to be constantly moving throughout their summer range in the Wrangell Mountains. The kids and I were anticipating a good hunt, allowing us the opportunity to share our harvest in the village.

We were climbing through the tundra and spotted a young bull caribou. We stopped and watched to see what he was going to do. We hoped he would stick around so we could plan a stalk.

The bull started to move in that peculiar caribou gait that can take them for miles without a rest. This particular bull traveled down and across a canyon then up the other side to a valley that seemed like it would be an easy stalk for us. We hoped he would stay put for a while. Would he still be there by the time we could get close enough to him?

"Laren, I think if we go over to that high point on that rocky ridge we can get a good shot at him if he stays in that canyon."

"Yeah, let's go get him," replied Laren.

We got to the top of the ridge and moved with great stealth. Kristi, Randy, and the four pack dogs stayed back out of sight. We made our way to the edge of the small canyon where Mr. Bull Caribou would be coming along.

"There he is, Dad!" Laren and I saw the bull at about the same time. I could feel the adrenalin flow and wondered how Laren would hold up. Our hearts were pounding wildly. We waited breathlessly, and Laren jacked a shell into the chamber of his rifle. I whispered, "It's about 200 yards, so hold dead on."

Laren was sitting and he aimed carefully. I thought, *He's had plenty of time to get steady and drop that bull.* I could see the 'bou flip his head and act nervous. I was sure he had winded or seen us, as he was looking right at us. He was about to leave.

Come on, Son, hurry or you'll lose this opportunity, I thought to myself. Finally, after what seemed an eternity, Laren said, "I'm ready." Later he told me that as he said this, he was thinking, *These cross hairs just will not settle and hold steady. Dang, I have to make a good shot. There, that'll do it. Now I'll squeeze carefully.*

At the crack of the rifle, we expected to see the bull drop, but he just stood there! Laren jammed another round in, and throwing caution to the wind, he fired again. This time the caribou dropped like a ton of bricks. We were elated, and I shook Laren's hand and said, "Hey, you got your first big game animal. Nice shot!"

Laren and his sister Kristi with Laren's first bull caribou

After dressing the bull, we returned to Kristi and Randy. We decided to make camp, and I would pack the bull to the vehicle and then come right back to the camp. The next day we would go on in to find a good ram or two.

Laren learns how to field dress a caribou.

Early the next morning we moved up the valley to sheep habitat. We were looking for a good base campsite when a young bull caribou dared us to put it down. Kristi accommodated him and ended up getting her first caribou. "Wow!" she exclaimed, after firing several shots and finally scoring, knocking the bull down. "I thought I could shoot more accurately than that," she said.

"You hit him two or three times," Randy replied. "That's not bad shooting."

Kristi's bull

We field-dressed Kristi's bull and then continued to look for a campsite. Not too much farther, we came to a beautiful little canyon with a bubbly mountain stream. It was a great spot for our base camp. We set the tent in as level a place as we could find. Then I set out four No.1 traps for parka squirrels. I planned on one squirrel for each pack dog per day.

Trapping squirrels for dog food saved us the weight problem of packing food for the dogs. The dogs were Alaskan huskies. They were beautiful animals and were strong and healthy, able to pack 40 to 45 pounds each. The stream sang its wilderness song to us as we finished setting up camp.

Base camp packed in on the dog's backs

The next day started early at 5 a.m. We left the camp set up for our home base. After our usual hearty breakfast of instant oatmeal, we packed each dog with the gear we'd need for the day. Then we set out for the day's adventure.

Our travel had taken us about 11 miles into rugged terrain well above the tree line. This was day three, and as we climbed we saw our first Dall sheep. We set up the spotting scope and watched the band of ewes and lambs. The lambs were frolicking in the early morning sunshine.

It was not too long until we spotted some rams about two miles away on a rocky precipice. We sat down on a bank of gravel known as a glacial moraine. We planned to stalk the rams and get close enough for a good shot.

The pack dogs were lying in our midst. One dog was to the left of Kristi and one was to the right, close to her head. The dogs were protective of their packs and jealous of Kristi. The dog on her left was aggressive and lunged at the dog on her right just behind her head.

Kristi threw her hand back to get out of the way and stand up, but her hand was in the path of the powerful jaws of the husky. The husky accidently bit Kristi as it snapped at the other dog.

She screamed and lunged to get away. Randy grabbed the collar of the dog nearest him, and I got hold of the other one. We stopped the dog fight and turned to doctor the bite on Kristi's hand.

Kristi had a skin-deep gash on the back of her hand alongside the middle tendon to her middle finger. I washed it carefully and put on some anti-bacterial medicine and a bandage from my first aid kit. It was painful, and we thought it probably was bruised as well as cut. Kristi assured us she was okay and wanted to keep hunting.

The rams were still in view. We decided to push on to complete our stalk. When we were about 350 yards below one of the rams, we could see that in order to get closer we would have to go a long ways around and climb up a steep rock strewn hillside. The chances of not being seen by the ram were not good.

We asked Kristi how she was feeling. She said she was doing fine. We thought she would be okay, since we were able to treat her wound so quickly and thoroughly. I had an excellent first aid kit, and I'd used a good antiseptic and had cleaned the wound carefully. The kids were as eager to get to the rams as I was, and Kristi was not in distress at this time.

Kristi was a hearty tomboy type. I can remember watching her run her horse full bore through rough terrain, fall off, and get back on, like a trick rider in a circus, as if nothing happened. She was one tough kid and never complained.

It was getting late in the afternoon, and it did not look too feasible to get closer to the rams without spending a lot of time circling and climbing above the sheep. I decided to try a shot with my 6 mm 100 grain cartridge. This .244 caliber bullet travels about 3000 feet per second and has a fairly flat trajectory. I set my pack on a rock to use as a rest, allowing me to shoot from a prone position.

After careful aim, I squeezed a round off. We heard the impact of the slug hit the ram and saw him crumple and roll down the chute below him. He rolled about 100 feet and hung up on a large rock. We watched him for a while to be sure he wasn't going to get up and run away. Satisfied that he was down for the count, we began the nearly vertical climb to the ram.

After arriving at the spot where the ram was hit, I gave my rifle to Randy, and worked my way down the chute to the ram. It was precarious going and a slip would send me down the mountain much faster than I cared to go. Nudging the ram off the rock and being careful to stay balanced, I watched the ram slip over the edge of the rock and tumble down the chute until it lay at the bottom.

At the bottom of the chute

Now I was in the chute and needed to get out without a slip. I thought, *Oh, boy, this is worse than it looked. I'm in deep trouble if I slip. The kids would be in a bad way if I get hurt.*

165

Carefully, I climbed out of the chute and gave a sigh of relief. We all made our way back down the cliff to the ram at the bottom of the chute where he lay in a much safer position.

I was glad Randy was with us. He was a skilled hunter and not your average high school senior. It was like having a competent adult man with me, and we could combine skills and knowledge to cope with the rigors of wilderness conditions.

We skinned and boned the sheep quickly and took time to cape the pelt, then packed up without delay.

Laren helps.

Finally the dogs were loaded with meat, and we had our gear plus the sheep cape. The first half mile was over a large field of talus rock. We picked our way through boulders of one to two feet in diameter. We had to be careful, however, and not overdo the dogs' endurance ability.

Laren obviously did not have the endurance of an adult, and his age and ability had to be considered. Kristi's injury was starting to hurt her more, and I could see she was getting worse. I was glad Randy was with me. I told the kids, "We better sit down and take a short break if we're going to get back to camp with any energy left at all."

While we were resting in the middle of a rock slide, I noted how steep and treacherous the footing was. It would be easy to sprain an ankle loaded like we were. I said, "We'd better be careful and not turn an ankle."

We had traversed down the mountain and came to a pass that dropped us over a ridge into the drainage where our base camp lay.

I said, "Boy, it'll be good to get back to camp and take a deep drink of that fresh spring water." The sun was setting, and the view looking west across the valley where Copper Lake lay glistening in the setting sun was one of those pictures that cannot be described. It was as if God opened the heavens and gave us a glimpse inside.

I wanted to take a picture. That's when I asked Laren to hand me the camera and discovered it was lost.

Laren looked at me with anguish in his eyes and said, "Dad, I lost the camera!" Laren had just presented us with our second major problem.

Now, the problem of a lost camera would not be so bad if it were a ten dollar throwaway camera that you buy at Wal-Mart, but this was an Olympus with an F1.5 lens, an expensive camera, indeed. This was one of those times that, as a father, I had a great opportunity. I could express the frustration I was feeling in a healthy way, or I could rake Laren over the coals and ruin our relationship. I could remember when I had done something just as costly and careless. This could have been me. I could see how easy it was to set the camera down and forget to pick it up.

In fact, I remembered when I was a 16-year-old on a deer hunt with my dad and an older hunter friend of his whom I respected. He was an expert gunsmith and muzzle loading barrel maker. In addition, he was a superb shot.

The short of it was, we had stopped to rest at a mountain spring when we were packing out three mule deer bucks on our three riding horses.

I had laid down my new Model 70, 30'06 Winchester rifle out of the way of the horses' feet. We let the horses drink first, and then we drank our fill of the cold liquid. It was a refreshing rest for a tired 16-year-old.

We picked up the lead ropes and continued down the mountain to our pickups, a jaunt of about three miles. When my dad asked me where my rifle was, I answered with a panic similar to what I saw now on Laren's face.

I remember the painful feeling of panic and embarrassment as I hiked back up the mountain to hopefully find my rifle before some other lucky hunter found it. To my great relief, it was right where I had left it. I will never forget how grateful I felt that day. I suspected Laren felt just as I did and would be self-incriminating enough and did not need my judgment.

It was my job to demonstrate calmness and trust in the Lord. I hoped I accomplished my objective. After a fast hike, I soon found myself back at the site of our sheep kill. I did not find the camera and was disappointed.

If I walked back the easiest route or just went back without thinking too much about it, then I might actually walk the route we had probably taken when we had left earlier. Who knows, I just might stumble onto it.

I started across the talus rock field in the fading light. I stopped where I thought we would have rested, and I was standing there thinking what an impossible task this was. I prayed, "Lord, show me where to look."

Not 50 feet away was a large rock that stood a bit above all the other rocks. Miraculously, there at the base of the rock sat the camera. In the dim light, I noticed that if I stood at any other location, I could not have seen the camera. It was indeed a miracle.

The kids saw me coming down the trail. They knew at once that I had been successful, as I had a spring to my step and a smile on my bearded face. What a lift for a heavy heart.

There is no way to describe our joy. I knew the trip was not over, and we still had a lot of obstacles in front of us. However, we had faith we would make it back to camp and out to the road where we had parked.

We continued on our way until it was so dark it was dangerous to continue our attempt to get back to our base camp. Randy found a huge boulder suspended on each end by other boulders, making a sort of cave to crawl into. There was not much room for four people, but the close quarters demanded we almost hug each other. This helped us stay warm, especially since our body heat could not escape up into the black night sky.

We huddled together until the moon came out about three hours later. I looked around and determined we could see well enough to travel safely. It was one of those gorgeous moonlit nights where one could see quite well. The northern lights were swirling around and seemed to be inviting us to be on the move. Knowing Kristi's condition, we were only too glad to accept the invitation.

About 3 a.m. we arrived at our base camp. We fell into bed knowing morning would come too soon. This time of year in late August, the day quietly breaks from gray to full light as early as 4 a.m. Needless to say, we stayed in our beds just a mite longer than the breaking of day.

Kristi was getting feverish, and after a quick breakfast, we packed the dog packs and our backpacks and checked the area for anything left. Everything looked okay. We headed down across the alpine turf, studded with small white blossoms on the mats of alpine phlox. It is amazing what beauty can be found in a microcosm of a square meter on the tundra.

On the way out the white sox flies were merciless. I could understand how the wilderness was a heartless teacher. How we responded was the difference between life and death at one extreme and between comfort and discomfort at the other end of the scenario.

We each cut a branch of a willow with leaves still on and used it for a switch to fan our faces so the bugs could not bite us so much. This was a trick shown to me by the Indians of our village. They call it a "benigee." In reality, I like a good insect spray with Deet in it, but with no spray available, a benigee is the ticket.

We wasted no time in loading the pickup when we arrived. I drove with a sense of urgency while the kids slept. Kristi slept fitfully as her fever was climbing and her hand was swelling with red streaks moving up her arm.

At Glennallen's Faith Hospital, to our surprise, the doctor immediately put Kristi into intensive care. She had tubes and needles in her arm and was administered antibiotics intravenously. She was one sick girl. In fact, we learned that she easily could have lost part of her hand or arm if we hadn't received medical attention when we did. I knew blood poisoning was serious, but I had no concept of how fast it can spread or how dangerous it really is.

I am reminded time and again of the provision of God. He is our sufficiency when He is our pilot. You do not have to be in the Alaska wilds to discover this truth. God cares for every person. He even showed His benevolence to us as we pursued our winter's meat supply.

On this trip we saw two huge problems erased by the Lord. The first problem was a dog bite, and the second was a lost camera. The problems were solved in such a way that the kids and I could see how God cares for us and loves us. What was really important was not that we successfully got game or found the camera, but that we traveled together and grew much closer to each other as a result of the experience.

◄►◆◄►◆◄►◆◄►◆◄►

The Master Leads
By Larry Roper

The Master leads us all along.
In cities too, yes, even among throngs.
In the wilderness we see clearly his leading each day.
Nothing to fear; just follow his leading all the way.

Chapter 14
Wilderness Rebuilds a Man

The day broke bright and clear. Our plans were made, and our gear was packed. We had a direction to go with a destination equaled only in our dreams. We had never been to this place before but had good instructions of how to get to the Dadina River gravel bar, a typical Alaskan bush airstrip. I had hunted nearby at the hourglass shaped, unnamed lake accessed from the Cheteslena River about 11 miles southeast. According to the map, the Dadina River route should be closer, and the airstrip was longer, a plus if heavily loaded, as we hoped to be.

I had seen moose near the lake on the Dadina side earlier in the year on a scouting trip with my friend and pilot, Scrib. We would soon know if we had picked the best drop-off location. My brother-in-law and longtime hunting partner, Gary, was the first to be ferried into the airstrip in a Super Cub modified to make it a full-fledged bush plane. It had oversized balloon tires and a stall kit on the wings. We had contracted with a bush pilot to fly us.

George, an Athabascan Indian friend and Alaskan hunting partner, would be flown in next. Then I would come with the balance of our equipment. The plan was to hike to the lake from the north side, hopefully to find one of the bulls I had seen earlier. We could then decide which airstrip was best to use.

We wanted to get a moose quickly and then hike the eight or nine miles up the Cheteslena River to Sheep Gulch, where we would get into some good trophy Dall sheep.

Gary was dropped off first by the pilot and had time to waste while he waited for George and me. It wasn't long before George arrived, and then I came in last. They were rested and ready to get on the trail.

It was 1977. My wife Betty, the children, and I were starting our second year as missionaries in Copper Center, Alaska. This was my second hunting season in Alaska, and it was important for me to get a moose to share with our Indian friends and parishioners. Unless you have lived in a Native village, it is difficult to understand what it means in terms of acceptance to be a good hunter and provide for your family and clan.

George waits for the next hunter.

The church in Copper Center was established by Vince and Becky Joy early in the 1940s. It was served by two elderly Native pastors and a missionary pastor to oversee the work and help the small church congregation be self-supporting and self-governing.

Our job was to teach, disciple, win the younger generation to Christ, and, in general, be all that we could be to both the white and Native populations in the Copper Center village. Role modeling and being with the people doing things their way plus letting them teach us how to cope with the Alaskan environment were the primary tools used to accomplish our mission.

George and I became good friends. Our friendship flourished because he could be himself and have his personal beliefs, and I could be me having my personal beliefs. By agreement, we didn't try to convert each other to our own personal belief system. This was okay with me since I had the objective of role modeling how to live as a Christian on a daily basis. In addition, it was the only way George would let me into his world. I still had the goal of seeing him come to know the Lord.

I believe some of my near tragedies in the bush and my success as a hunter and fisherman were instrumental in our missionary work. For example, hunting was the only door open for me to establish a relationship with George. This door was opened in an unusual way.

I had heard that George hated missionaries, but I also had heard that he was one of the better Indian hunters in the area. This piqued my interest, and I was determined to get acquainted. One day I decided to go visit him. I was somewhat worried, based on what I had heard. In my mind I could see George running me off.

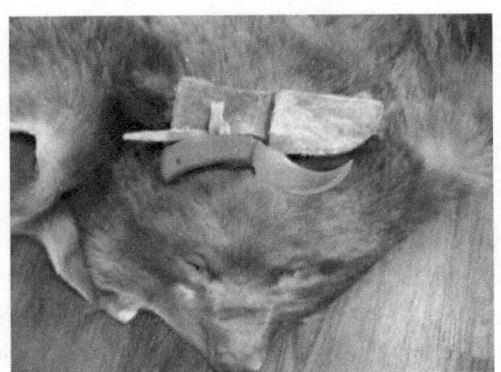

Skinning knife made by George

He was a big guy and perceived as intimidating. My mind was racing with negative ideas. I thought, *I wonder if I'll be thrown out. What if he threatens me? What should I do? Well, here goes nothing. I always did like the direct approach.*

I knocked on the door of George's cabin and he said, "Come in." I opened the door and stepped inside. He was at a workbench carving a seal. He made knives, carved Alaskan wildlife, and worked with rawhide.

He was an excellent craftsman. I was able to establish rapport with George by being direct. I said, "I heard you don't like missionaries, and I am one. I'm probably cut from a different cloth than you've seen before now." I thought to myself, *Well, if he doesn't like this approach, then I've blown my attempt to get acquainted.*

Even though I felt trepidation, I believed God had directed me this far. So I plunged ahead. I said, "I'm a former wildlife biologist, and I love to hunt and fish. I've heard you're the best hunter in the area, so I figure you're the guy I need to know." *I suppose he thinks I'm a real nut*, I thought, but I plunged on and we soon had a good conversation going. We cooked up a hunting trip right away. The Lord was in this, for sure, and the trip strengthened our friendship.

We went ptarmigan hunting in the Summit Lake area in early spring. We were on snowshoes and came to a steep hillside falling away from us. We were standing on a small cornice overlooking the Gulkana River. The slope was about 300 feet to the bottom.

As we stood there catching our breath and enjoying the beauty of the scene, the snow sagged with an abrupt soft sound. The entire slab of snow, which was about 50 feet wide and 100 feet long by 4 feet deep, slipped down into the valley below.

Unbelievably, without any movement on our part, George and I were caught in the small avalanche. We were whipped down the slope at incredible speed. Somehow we were able to stay erect, although we were up to our waists in snow. The snow dust filled the air around us, and we had trouble staying oriented.

We came to an abrupt stop, but we'd lost track of each other. As the snow dust settled, I saw that George was in the same predicament as I. We were both up to our waist in snow packed so tight it was like concrete about half set up. Furiously, we began to dig ourselves out before the snow locked us in. We were able to get free of the snow, and we looked around in amazement. We still had our shotguns and packs and felt good about not being buried under the snow, which could have been fatal for us.

Could it be that God's voice was the whisper that started the avalanche? I believe this event gave George and me a special kinship. It was the first step in George's seeing the love of God.

Our bond was tested a few years later when George and his wife had a physical fight in the local bar. She called Betty, sobbing, and asked Betty to come take her home. Betty picked her up, and in the meantime, I drove my pickup to the bar to see if I could help George and in the process help them both.

I drove into the gravel parking lot and saw George wandering aimlessly around the lot appearing to be looking for something. I walked right up to George and said, "Hi!" He looked up, cocked his fist, and was going to hit me. I said, "George! It's Larry!"

"Oh," he said. "What do you want?"

"I came to help you if I could."

George looked at me through myopic vision. "Well, you could help me find my glasses. I can barely see."

That night took a new turn in our relationship. George and I sat in the bar, which was a surprise to him that a missionary would be in such an unholy place. We talked until near midnight or after. I ended up driving him to Pump 12 on the Alyeska oil pipeline construction camp, where he worked and had to go on shift at 6 a.m.

The next thing we knew, we cooked up a moose hunt in the Dadina River drainage. My brother-in-law Gary, from Colorado, wanted to hunt moose with his bow, so we included him in our plans.

Here we were, the result of plans made in a bar. We were hiking through the muskeg with 45- to 50-pound packs, which was not an easy task. The fact was, it could wear a person out. I noticed George kept lagging behind, and we had to wait longer and longer for him. He was sweating profusely, and he was holding us up. We would not make it to the lake by dark.

Gary and I would walk and then wait. Finally the waits were longer than the times of travel. We all three talked it over and decided mutually that Gary and I would go ahead, set up camp, and fix supper for us. It occurred to me that George might be trying to dry out cold turkey (stop drinking all at once) and was using this trip as a means to that end.

I knew George was a good woodsman, but I was still worried when he hadn't joined us by evening. It would be lights out soon, so Gary and I ate our tasty snack of crackers and jam, rolled up in our sleeping bags, and were soon fast asleep.

I prayed the Lord would intervene and keep George safe. He needed help to dry out from the ravages of alcohol abuse without going through the DTs. The DTs, or delirium tremors, are devastating. It causes hallucinations, pain, shakes, and extreme weakness. In severe cases, blackouts can occur that may lead to death.

I was really concerned. I didn't know at the time, but George had been on a two- or three-month drinking binge. Now here we were in the wilderness with no medical facility. George could be in real trouble.

We decided it had to be George's problem. We could only do so much.

We could keep a close watch on him, but we'd let him take his time to recover his strength. His pride was such that I think he wanted us not to witness his drying out.

George and Gary on the airstrip

The next morning we still saw nothing of George. We ate quickly and packed down to the Cheteslena River airstrip to look for him. We broke out from the underbrush, and there in the middle of the airstrip was George's tent.

He was still asleep, but we had no qualms about waking him. Sullenly, George got up and packed his gear, and we went up the trail leaving the airstrip behind. We didn't say much or ask why George had elected to stay down on the river bottom.

It was there on the airstrip that I got some indication that Gary thought I had pulled a real boner asking George to hunt with us. However, as it turned out, Gary played a vital role in the rebuilding of George's outlook on life and subsequent submitting of his life to the Lord. This did occur, but it was much later in George's life.

As time progressed, Gary and George became friends and the tension was gone. We all three had good camaraderie. The secret was not to force anything but give time and the wilderness a chance to work.

We climbed up a moose trail headed in the direction of the hourglass shaped lake. We had wasted at least a half day when we could have been hunting, so we struck off as fast as we could.

Now we knew we should have come in via the Cheteslena airstrip instead of the Dadina route. The trail led us into a draw about a half mile from the lake, and we decided to set our base camp in the draw. It was hidden amongst high alders and was not a good campsite. Level ground was hard to find. We were in drainage, and a major rainstorm could drown us out. But worst of all, a bear could approach without our seeing it.

The camp was not in the best site.

Since we were in a hurry, we justified our site selection. We had good running water and three fairly level spots for each tent. We could move if we found a better site as we got acquainted with the area.

We set up camp and ate a quick lunch so we could go on an afternoon scout and moose hunt. We split up, with each of us taking a different direction. I chose to drop down below the lake on the south side and look for moose sign.

Sneaking along through buffalo berry brush and scattered taiga spruce, I began to see a lot of moose droppings, indicating there were moose frequenting the area. I was in a hunting mode of behavior, stopping every two to three soft steps, dissecting every shadow and nook and cranny in the habitat.

I saw a flash of white. Carefully, I set down my Ruger Number One .270 Winchester and dug out my binoculars from inside my shirt where they were hanging around my neck. Focusing on the brush amidst the spruce grove, I saw the white object swing toward me. It was the palm of an antler of a mature bull moose. The distance was about 125 to 130 yards. I thought, *Aha! I have you now, big boy!* This is what hunting is all about: a good stalk and a controlled adrenalin rush, which is an ability learned over time that produces calmness while still being excited.

The brush was too high for a sitting or a prone shot, so I used the branch of a high bush cranberry about shoulder high. It was not the steadiest rifle rest, but it was better than offhand shooting. The cross hairs of my 2 x 7 power Leopold Golden Ring scope settled just behind the shoulder. I squeezed off a shot. I heard the bullet hit, but to my surprise, the bull just stood there.

Darn, maybe the .270 was a bit small for a critter as big as a moose. There was a lot of hide, muscle, and bone to penetrate. I put in another round and placed another 150 grain Nosler in the lungs.

The magnificent bull took two steps forward and collapsed. I rejoiced and thought of the Psalm where it says the Lord owns the cattle on a thousand hills and He cares for them and He cares for me.

Now we had meat for the coming winter season. However, there was just one small detail: This was plus or minus 700 pounds of moose meat that must be boned and packed out to the Cheteslena airstrip. Once we got all the meat home we would cut it up, package it, and store it in the freezer. Not a small detail, when one stops to think about it.

First, the bull needed to be skinned, and I began the arduous job. An hour later the work was done. I began to bone the meat and carry it to a spot a few feet away, where I covered it with brush and prayed that if a grizzly or wolf came to the kill, he would work on the skeleton and the gut pile first.

I had learned that it was nearly impossible to keep a bear from a kill, but you just might get him to work on the part of the moose you did not want. I stood there looking at the skeleton and the entrails, which in this case were still contained within the skeleton. It looked like good bear bait.

The bull was on his brisket and lay pretty much in a vertical position. I just left him that way. He was a nice big bull and had a 55-inch spread of decadent antlers. (Decadence is an indicator that he was an older bull, and his antlers were regressing and becoming more spindly each subsequent year, except for the base diameter, which continues to get larger each year.)

When I skinned him, I made an incision down the back bone from ear to tail and then peeled the skin from the carcass, leaving a clean hide on each side to place the boned meat.

The meat was then put in bags small enough to handle and carry away from the immediate site. For one man to handle a moose was at least a half day of work, and that doesn't include packing it out. For that job, two men need at least three days.

After I'd skinned the moose and moved the meat, I headed back to camp to meet George and Gary. They had not seen any game but had gotten acquainted with some of the terrain.

The next morning at daybreak George decided to hunt northwest of the lake, while Gary and I decided to go below the lake. We hunted through the day and did not see any moose; however, early that morning we stopped on a point overlooking the lake and I pointed out my moose kill.

Much to our surprise, standing beside the moose carcass was a good-sized gray wolf. The distance was about a half mile. The wolf picked up our movement and slinked into the brush. It gave me the sense that there was a lot more going on in the wilderness than meets the eye. We didn't see any game the rest of the day.

Gary and I arrived back in camp before George and set about preparing a meal from freeze dried food.

When George showed up, he had an interesting story to tell. He said, "I forgot to take anything to eat this morning. I had been hunting from early morning into the afternoon. I felt weak and starved. I have not been able to eat enough for the last two or three days. I was sick at my stomach and at the end of my endurance. I was in this condition when I stumbled onto your moose kill. I had sat down to rest and heard an airplane. It circled a couple of times, and then the pilot dropped a package out the window, wagged his wings, and left. I walked over and picked up the package. Wow, it was full of brownies! I ate all of them!" It was obvious George did not think about for whom they were intended. He said, "The brownies were sure good, and I figured possession meant ownership for me."

We laughed and I said, "It was manna from heaven just for you, George!" We suggested that God was taking care of him. We left it at that and made plans for the next day's hunt. Little did we know, but the brownies were from Harriet, Gary's wife, and were meant for us to share. Scrib, my friend and pilot, had volunteered to drop them off and check us out from the air to let the families know we were okay. I believe this was the Lord's way of using this hunting trip to reach out to George, that he might believe. It was another seed planted.

We discussed our next move, and I proposed that since I had a moose, I would go up the North Fork of the Cheteslena River to Sheep Gulch and get a sheep, if possible. Then I would come back and help George and Gary get meat packed out. They might get something, or we could pack my moose to the airstrip.

They agreed, and I packed supplies for the two days. I made my way the eight or nine miles to Sheep Gulch, a tributary of the main Cheteslena River. The trail was good and I made good time. Later that morning, high in the gulch, I spotted a lone ram on a slope about three-fourths of a mile away. I dug out my 20-power spotting scope and determined he was a ram with about a seven-eighths or possibly a full curl.

I began the climb and eventually got within about 500 yards of the sheep. It was obvious that the rest of the way to the sheep was completely exposed, and there was no chance of a good stalk. The sheep was lying down looking my way. I waited several minutes, and then I decided to ask the Lord to turn the sheep around so he would be looking away from me. Then, if the Lord willed, I would hurry up and close the distance for a killing shot. I said, "Amen, Thy will be done."

A minute or two went by, and the ram stood up, stretched, urinated, and lay back down, but this time he lay down looking away from me, just as I had prayed. "Wow! Thank you, Lord!" Now what natural born wild sheep is going to stand up and turn and look in the direction that it has no open view? Sheep have eyes that are equal to our 8-power binoculars. That's pretty good vision, but it demands distances to view. I realized that what had just happened was a direct answer to my prayer.

A near miss

Quietly, I got up and walked as carefully as I could on the trail that led to the sheep. At about 200 yards the sheep jumped up and looked right at me. I froze in my position, and we began a stare down. I slowly dropped to a kneeling position, took aim, and shot. I missed. The sheep took off running from my right to left.

I knew the jig was up and no holds were barred. Caution was no longer needed, and I loaded another round into the .270 and took a quick shot. The ram dropped immediately. It truly was a gift, because I hit the ram in the neck while it was running at about 250 yards. A tough shot to make. It demonstrated to me that the Lord had directed the bullet.

I cleaned the ram and de-boned all the edible meat, then packed it in my backpack. I put the cape and head on top of the pack.

I made it back down the gulch to an unnamed creek now running too full for a safe crossing due to the glacier melting during the heat of the day.

It seemed obvious that a traveler would need to cross early in the morning when it would be running with less water. It was not the perfect place to camp since it was bear country. Making camp, I noticed a lot of bear sign, so I hung my pots and pans from limbs all around me. I moved the meat off to the side, leaving it in my pack. Dried salmon was my supper, then I turned my tired body in to bed, after saying a short prayer for safety.

The next morning the creek was down to a crossable depth. I donned my pack after a quick breakfast and walked to the creek. Fresh bear dung was steaming not 30 yards away from where I had slept soundly. Obviously, the Lord had protected me.

I crossed the creek and hiked the eight miles to the airstrip with no further incident. I saw two nice bull caribou about three or four miles from the airstrip. I cached the ram in the tree cache built to keep meat away from bears. It was located adjacent to a good camp spot next to the rough runway. The cache was a small log house built on top of a platform about fifteen feet in the air. The ladder was left on the ground in plain sight to be used by whoever needed to use the cache.

Back at the moose camp, I met George and Gary. We compared notes and laughed about the bear dung so close to my camp. Gary had passed up a bull of tremendous size. He could have taken this bull easily with a rifle. However, he was hunting with his bow. Although it was close, he let it go as it did not present a good broadside shot. As it was, they stared each other down at about 20 yards. Gary was satisfied and felt his personal hunting ethic was intact, since his hunting ability allowed him to get within bow range. It was just circumstances that kept him from scoring that day. He would never forget the experience of being so close to such a large animal.

The cache that is bear proof

George had not been successful, but was happy to help pack my meat to the airstrip. He knew we would share the meat. I suspected that he was pretty sick and not at full strength. Wisely, he took it easy and let his body recover from heavy drinking.

A week in the wilderness had come and gone. We were ready to be flown back to civilization and our families. All the meat was ferried to the airstrip, and the camp was moved to a protected site near the gravel bar. All we needed was for our pilot to arrive. There was just one complication. The wind had begun to blow a gale. By Alaska standards, this is better than 50 to 60 mph.

On the second day of the blow, with no abating of the wind, we heard an airplane overhead. As we stood there and watched, to our surprise, the plane dropped onto the gravel bar. Going much too fast, it careened down the makeshift runway and at the end, spun around dangerously in the willows and came back our way.

The pilot pulled up, jumped out of his plane, and gave us a "howdy." He then tied the wings down to willow bushes. We asked what on earth he was doing flying in that kind of weather. We wondered why he'd landed with such cavalier speed that required a spin at the end of the runway. His cocky answer was, "Airplanes were made to fly in the wind and I had to land that way because I had no brakes."

George and Larry in moose camp

Gary was there, too, and he fixed supper.

This daring bush pilot was Jake. We nicknamed him "Grizzly" Jake after listening to his many stories of flying in the Alaskan bush to hunt. He stayed in camp with us the next two days, and

184

as a result we ran out of food. We had plenty of meat, so we broiled shish kebabs of moose and sheep tenderloin. The menu was sheep for breakfast, moose for lunch, and sheep or moose for supper. We also found a couple of cans of cream-style corn in the tree cache.

Grizzly Jake took off the next day during a lull of the wind, and we were left alone to wait for our plane to shuttle us out and back to our families.

Toward evening of the third day the wind abated. The next morning when our pilot returned, he was pretty grumpy. When we confronted him over his manner, he said, "That redhead's wife nearly drove me crazy."

Apparently, Gary's wife had called him several times a day requesting that he fly in and get us. She felt she needed to keep asking so he wouldn't put the job of getting us at a low priority. She had three small children and couldn't help but worry about Gary's safety.

Looking back on the hunt, we could see God at work in each of our lives. George had food provided when he needed it, and he saw how I was protected by the Lord from bears. Gary saw how God would keep us on the ground when it was unsafe to fly. Years later, I saw the results of the seed planted when George became a believer and trusted in the Lord for his salvation.

I do believe the winds that kept us at bay were just another intervention by God. In His all-knowing insight, He knew George was not ready to come out of the wilderness. He knew we all needed a bit more time in the Cheteslena. I believe George needed a little more time to be with two guys who loved the Lord and were not afraid to say so. The hunt was over, and we knew George had seen God's love in his life. The wilderness was the tool for rebuilding George after a long binge of heavy drinking.

About the Authors

Betty and Larry pray the Lord guides you all the way

Betty and Larry have been married over 50 years, and they love the outdoors.

Larry has said that he looks at himself and he wonders what it is that makes him tick. He said to me, "How did I get this way? Was I born to be a hunter? Is it just because this is the way the twig was bent?"

He grew up with a dad who worked hard, played hard, and took care of his family. His dad hunted, fished, and provided horses from the time he could remember. Larry played in sports in high school and it was there that he met Betty in his senior year. She was pretty and vivacious and would fish and hunt with him.

Betty grew up in a home with two sisters. Her dad was a life-long railroad man who took good care of his family. They went on picnics and spent time swimming and playing sports. Betty was a drill team leader and earned a 4.0 GPA in high school and in college. Betty had a National Merit Scholarship award for full tuition for four years at the college of her choice.

Larry and Betty dated for three years, then got married and continued to go to college together. It was during this time that they both began to live for the Lord and let Him guide them toward their future destiny.

They finished college and Larry took a job as a conservation officer in Utah. They also began a family when their first child, Kristi, was born in 1962. A career change to the U.S. Forest Service came next, as did two more children, Lori in 1964 and Laren, Jr., in 1966.

Restless for more knowledge and the leading of the Lord, Larry entered a master of science program in forest science at the University of Idaho. This led to wildlife research in Kremmling, Colorado, for the Colorado Division of Wildlife.

After six years in Colorado, back to school to seminary was the marching orders for both Larry and Betty. They prepared themselves for the ministry and followed it up as missionaries with Send, International, in the Alaska Division. From there they took more training, and Larry obtained a Ph.D. in Christian counseling. They started a Christian counseling ministry in northwestern Colorado and eventually moved the ministry to Scottsbluff, Nebraska. They also lived on and farmed a 160-acre farm in the area.

Along the way they were active in a lot of outdoor activities. They hunted, fished, showed horses, and raised dogs and quarter horses. Miscellaneous small farm livestock and 4H for the kids also were part of their experiences.

Larry and Betty are now retired and wanted to share some of their experiences. They hope you enjoy reading about them as much as they have enjoyed living and writing about them.

How the Twig Was Bent
By Larry Roper

I was thinking about life and how it has been spent.
I think I lived according to the way the twig was bent.
How was it bent and who did the trick?
Mom was instrumental as she gave me much to make me tick.
Dad was part of the equation, too, showing a lot to me.
Often I do a job and step back for him to see.

Then reality says, he has been gone for some time,
e'en tho' his presence I do feel.
My wife is constant wisdom for me,
just like the spokes in the wheel.
Others have had influence along the way,
not one so dominant that I should say.

Me, I left out, and don't dare to talk,
'cause, you would see, I went the way I really wanted to walk.
Now God has cause to give us a smile.
It was He who gave us life worthwhile.
It was He who brought the twig to life.
It was He who used many to bend it with a bit of strife.

You probably wonder why I tell these thoughts so true.
Well, it is so we can accept ourselves
and what we have had to do.
Then share your tale with someone else today.
Tell it with a twinkle in your eye,
knowing the way we are bent is His way.

Epilogue

We have written this book with the intent of showing, by sharing these stories of our hunting and fishing adventures, how God works in each of our lives. We do not believe we need something miraculous to prove God is at work in us and through us. He is with us in our grandest moments when the entire world would praise His name. He is also with us in the smallest of whispers and in the darkest hours of our lives.

It is our desire that these stories of events occurring in our lives would inspire the readers to look at their own lives differently. It seems to be human nature that when we look at someone else, it is easy to say God sure answered prayer, but when we look at ourselves we tend to minimize the importance of the way God is at work in us. Therefore, we pray that each reader will realize God loves us and we need to give Him the credit for all He does in our lives.

We believe that wilderness outings and hunts for subsistence have given our family backbone and have provided the foundation for us to become bonded together. This has carried down to the fourth and fifth generations. It all started as far back as my Grandfather Roper's hunts with his brothers during the Colorado gold rush days.

Our grandson Danny Hughes wrote the following short paper for his class in the ninth grade. In his own words and without adult prompting, he captures the essence of this message.

◀▶◆◀▶◆◀▶◆◀▶◆◀▶

Ever since I was a little kid there have always been two things I have loved: hunting and spending time with my Grandpa Roper and since my grandpa also loves hunting, on many occasions I have got to do both at the same time. When we lived in Colorado one of our favorite things to do was go cottontail rabbit hunting. We would go out with our .22's and traipse around the hillsides in search of those "wascally wabbits."

Whenever I shot one he would call me "Dead-Eye Dan." When I was 12 years old he took me for a three-day pack trip on horses to scout out our elk hunting grounds. Hunting and riding horses is what we loved to do.

Dan and Grandpa scout for elk.

When he moved to Nebraska and I moved to Alaska our hunting trips were now very few and far between, but the Christmas of 1999 I got to go visit Grandpa and guess what we did? You got it, we went goose hunting. Here's how it got.

He came into the room to wake me up at six o'clock. I was very excited as I always am about hunting so I got up, got dressed, and went upstairs to join Grandpa for breakfast. We each had a bowl of cereal, a banana and a glass of orange juice.

Then we put on our camouflage, got the shotguns, our ammo and the goose calls (I had been practicing my calling the day before), and we headed out in his diesel truck just before the break of dawn. It was about six-thirty; we had just enough time to move the decoys to the corn field we wanted them in.

We loaded the decoys in the back of Grandpa's truck then we drove to the field and unloaded them. Then Grandpa hid the truck behind a hill while I arranged the decoys in a fish hook shape. The geese are supposed to land right in the middle of the curve. When Grandpa got back he helped me finish. Next we took the two chair decoys with seats in them and put them in good shooting positions. At about seven-thirty we crawled into our decoy blinds and were just in time because the geese had just started to fly over our heads.

My grandpa's farm is about a mile away from Lake Minatare Wildlife Refuge where the geese sleep for the night then head out for the farm fields for the day to feed.

The geese fly from the lake from about seven-thirty to nine-thirty. So our plan was to call in the decoys for about two hours and try to coax the birds into landing. Well we sat there calling those birds while literally flocks of geese flew over our heads. There was much more honking going on than at a New Jersey turnpike. But the birds didn't seem the least bit interested.

Then finally a group of about twelve that my grandpa was calling at turned and headed straight for us. The adrenaline started flowing through my veins as they got closer and set their wings to land. I reach down for my shotgun and then the geese flew away. Something just didn't look right to them I guess.

"Oh well, we'll just have to keep trying," Grandpa said. So we did; we kept calling and calling and nothing came in. It was about nine-fifteen and I was about to give up all hope, but all of a sudden we heard some honking from somewhere. We couldn't see them but we knew they were close. So Grandpa started calling with all his heart.

Dan got his goose.

Then I saw them flying towards us from the left. Two geese had committed to land; I was sure of it. They set their wings and flew in lower. They circled once and came in for the landing, and just after they started hovering like they do before they come down to the ground Grandpa yelled, "Take 'em!" So I flipped up my lid, raised my gun, took two shots and a goose fell out of the sky.

Grandpa and I were so happy that our hunt was a success. After I shot the goose we stayed for a few more minutes then went home to show Grandma, and for lunch we had smoked goose.

By Danny Hughes

◀▶◆◀▶◆◀▶◆◀▶◆◀▶

This story is not altered, edited, or changed from the way Danny put the tale down in writing. I believe it illustrates the value of quality outdoor experiences for our families and youth of America. Danny is now married and has three children. He is an EMT—Paramedic. Helping people is his vocational goal. Did outdoor experiences help Dan become the good citizen he is today?

These stories are true and have been the result of our hunting, fishing, and camping in self-guided adventures. These exploits were the result of researching the country using quality maps and acquiring the necessary equipment. We caution the average or beginning hunter to not try to duplicate these wilderness experiences unless you have the skills, patience, and equipment. This is the reason competent guides stay in business. They make the difference in going safely and with minimum investment of time and cost. A good guide and outfitter is perhaps the safest and least costly way of getting a true wilderness experience.

I Thessalonians 5:16-18 (NASB) says: "Rejoice always, pray without ceasing; in everything give thanks; for this is God's will for you in Christ Jesus." Open your heart, take Him in, and live. Live the reality of the risen Savior in your life today. May God bless you in all you do!

SEE YA!

In Memory. . .

Our friend and pilot, Larry Scribner

Special thanks and praise go to the families of Larry (Scrib) Scribner and Dean Wilson. These courageous men have completed their tour on this earth and are now and forever with the Lord. We miss them.

APPENDIX

Some pictures say a thousand words...

Copper Center Chapel

Pastor Jim McKinley, Traditional Chief

Martha sings

Glacier country

Larry reminisces

Dad and Laren get a tree

Larry and Pastor Jim McKinley in Valdez

The oil pipeline

Wilbur and Marilyn study the Bible with Larry and Betty

A big bull elk

Laren poses on the 54 Mile hunt

Dad packing, which was copied by Larry

Larry packs out a bull.

Randy knew where he wanted to go.

A caribou runs.

David, our nephew, was successful.

Sheep country

My back will heal

A big one

Betty fishes

Larry catches a big one.

The kids show a fish wheel.

Dad and Lori with Dad's first fish

Mom and Dad's bed on wheels

Typical taiga forest

Family moose hunt—we start out in the morning

Family moose hunt—we take a coffee break

That's all Folks!

I couldn't put the book down! As a child I spent many hours seated on a knee enthralled by Grandpa Roper's tales of hunting adventure. It was like the book itself was saying "Hey Danny, did I ever tell you about the time...?" This book was like a time machine transporting me back and it produced a very nostalgic feeling as I turned the pages. These true stories, along with countless hours of time invested in my outdoor education are part of what makes me who I am, and keeps me in pursuit of what I hope to be. This book will always be a treasure to me. Thanks Grandpa.

Daniel Hughes